The Sundown Trail

© Marc Alexander

ISBN 978-1-909473-17-1

Text prepared by www.willowebooks.org.uk

The Sundown Trail

by

Marc Alexander

Published by Willow Books

For David Leader

CHAPTER ONE

The wasteland shimmered sickly under the glare of the noon sun. Cursing it, the boy with the hoe straightened his aching back. He lifted his sullen gaze from the arid ground he had been trying to break and flicked back the dark blond hair which fell over his forehead like untidy thatch.

"Goddam it all to hell," he muttered, and emphasised his disgust with his surroundings by spitting accurately at a small white scorpion zig-zagging towards his heavy farm boot. Then his pale blue eyes focused on a tiny point of quicksilver glinting in a patch of Indian corn a few yards away. Grateful for an excuse to break the boredom of his labour, he approached the withered leaves and stalks which rustled metallically in heated air gusting from the desert.

As he reached the first rank of maize he stopped dead. The flash which had attracted him was the sun reflected from the octagonal barrel of a brass-framed Henry rifle.

"Do nothing, anglo, or you are likely to become very dead," the crouching owner of the gun commanded softly.

Whatever he may have felt at being confronted with a gun, no emotion appeared on the boy's tanned features.

"You gotta watch them Henry's," he drawled at length. "They got a bad habit of breakin' their firin' pins."

The man laughed shortly.

"I'm glad you are a cool one, anglo," he said with a slight Spanish accent. "Keep that way and you will have no trouble. I just want you to carry on as you were. Just hoe the ground and keep your lip buttoned. That way you'll live to see the sunset."

"I ain't gonna argue with a Henry pointin' at my belly," replied the boy. "But I can't help bein' kinda curious..."

"Let's just say I've had a bit of trouble and I'm waiting for my amigo. And let's also say I don't want to be noticed."

The boy laughed.

"There ain't none round here to notice you, *compadre.* My Pa's too drunk an' my Ma – why, she's too busy singin' hymns. Ain't no one else."

As he spoke the boy was looking carefully at the man with the gun. Obviously a Mexican, his features were olive and handsome, and his black-brown eyes shone with a cruel boldness which told the boy he would not hesitate to put any threat into practice.

"Back to work, anglo," he ordered. "Do not forget the Angel of Death is close."

The boy grunted, spat again to show he didn't really care and went back to where he had flung down his hoe. He poised the blade over the dry soil ready for the downward thrust, then paused and gazed at the maize which was now a blank wall of faded green.

"Say, *compadre,* if you're a bandit or sumpin' I'd sure like to join your outfit. Be better than bustin' these goddam clods..."

There was no spoken reply, but the boy saw the maize stalks sway as the rifle barrel was moved to and fro warningly.

"Ain't overloaded with humour," muttered the boy. "I'll jus' shut up." He drove the hoe viciously into the earth.

During the afternoon the boy worked in silence, always conscious of the hidden Mexican and the rifle which he instinctively knew followed his every movement. To his own surprise he did not feel any great personal fear. "He ain't got no quarrel with a nothin' like me," he thought. "I'll be all right so long as that Henry don't go off by accident. I'd never trust a Henry –" He came to realise he welcomed this drama as a break in the monotony which had clouded his life ever since he could remember.

Reaching the end of a row the boy looked up and surveyed the trail which wound past him and across the plain to where two flat-topped buttes of red rock soared majestically. Not far from where the trail emerged from the narrow gap between the two great formations, a cluster of shacks sagged dispiritedly. This miserable settlement and the desert was the only world he could really remember, and it was a world he hated. There had been a time, years ago, when the sun-warped buildings had been new and were expected to blossom into a prosperous trail-side settlement. That was when his father had come, had put up the biggest building of them all, and painted on the long board above the verandah "Red Buttes Provision and General Store." Now all that remained of the legend was a few peeling letters on the bleached wood.

The boy wiped the sweat from his forehead and resumed his task. It was unrewarding for here the desert began and it was an endless battle to grow crops to support his family and their few skinny animals.

Late in the afternoon he was struck by a sad thought. At any moment the Mexican's friend might come along and they would go off together on their mysterious business... and he would be left alone.

* * *

It was the chink of steel on rock which made

3

the boy glance up, and for the rest of his life he was to carry that first glimpse of the tall stranger riding along the trail towards him. So alien was he to the men the boy had known that, in the lurid light of the dying sun, he looked unreal – and splendid.

He was astride a large black gelding, and everything he wore, from his hat with the wide turned-down brim to his soft leather riding boots, was black under a toning of alkali dust. The only hint of vanity in the sombre outfit came from a snake-skin hatband. Blankets and slicker were in a neat roll strapped behind him and a Winchester hung from his saddle in its boot, balancing a large water canteen.

With a strange thrill, the boy saw the white bone handle of a revolver strapped low on each thigh. A two-gun man! Obviously here was the man that the Mexican had been waiting for.

The stranger raised his head to look at the boy, his face appearing suddenly from the shadow which had been cast by the hat. A dark moustache curved from above his compressed mouth and flowed down almost to his jawline, but it was his eyes that startled the boy. For a moment it seemed as though they were a pair of green stars. Then he realised the stranger was wearing tinted spectacles to protect his eyes against the dazzle of the wilderness.

Above the soft, endless swish of the dry maize came a faint rustle to the ears of the boy. It could have been made by a man shifting his weight from a cramped position, perhaps raising a rifle...

Suddenly he knew the truth, and felt aghast he had not been aware of it all along. The Mexican was not waiting for a fellow desperado, he was waiting to murder the stranger who even at this moment must be riding into the sights of the Henry rifle.

"Look out, mister," the boy screamed, dropping

4

the hoe and running towards the trail. "There's a fella in the maize patch with a gun."

At his high-pitched words the gelding halted, then reared nervously. Its sudden movement saved the stranger as, before the boy could yell another word, the concealed rifle exploded. The slug which had been destined for the black-garbed body of the stranger merely ripped his trouser leg and left a bloody weal along the flank of the horse.

Expecting to feel the next bullet shatter his back, the boy dived forward and lay full length in the ground he had broken up through the long afternoon. Sprawled prone, with his chin pressed into the dirt, he watched fascinated as the stranger slid back over the rump of his plunging mount. The animal skittered away, leaving its master crouched on the balls of his feet in the middle of the trail, a Colt Peacemaker in either hand.

The Henry cracked again and the stranger began to return the fire fast. The noise of the revolver and rifle blended together as the bullets whistled above the body of the boy. Everything had happened so quickly that he had not had time to feel fear. He watched, as though in a dream, as the stranger fired his right-hand gun at the sniper hidden in the maize.

He did not use both guns at once, but held the left gun loosely at his side. Then, as the hammer fell on the final cartridge in the first gun he made a movement which was the most beautiful the boy had ever seen. With a strange grace the emptied Colt dropped away from the man's right hand, leaving the fingers outstretched. At the same time his left hand threw the gun sideways across his body so it landed with its butt snugly in the open palm of the right. The fingers closed and the firing continued. It had been a perfect "border shift," done without the stranger moving his gaze from his enemy.

There was a cry from the corn. The boy rolled over, to look behind him and saw the Mexican stagger forward from his cover. The Henry had been dropped. He now had a silver pistol in his hand which spat flame wildly at the stranger. The last bullet from his dying gun threw up a spurt of earth a couple of yards in front of his feet. At every explosion of the stranger's Peacemaker his body jerked grotesquely like a marionette whose strings are plucked by a child. He dropped to his knees, his head thrown back and his face an agonised mask in the orange light, then pitched forward.

The following silence was as dramatic as the first salvo of shots. The boy slowly climbed to his feet, automatically brushing his dirtied hair from his eyes. Surrounded by a drifting cloud of powder smoke, the stranger stood in the middle of the trail, then slowly walked towards the Mexican, his gun trained on the inert body all the time. Reaching him he bent down over the bloodied body, and assured that life was extinct, slowly straightened up.

"Messy," he commented.

Without needing to look at what he was doing, his fingers deftly swung out the cylinder of the Colt and he began to reload. Speechlessly the boy came and stood beside him, looking down with a sickened curiosity at the corpse. It was obvious from the patches of blood that several of the stranger's .45 bullets had found their mark. For a moment the boy felt the vomit rise to his throat, he turned away and choked back his nausea.

"Say, mister," he began shakily at length, "I didn't know there could be shootin' like that. The way you did that shift... I thought it was just a tale that it could be done ..."

"It weren't that good," the stranger muttered in a drowsy voice. "There shouldn't have been any need for the shift. Once ..." He suddenly seemed to recollect himself, and, turning to the boy, said: "Guess I gotta thank you for the warnin'. When I saw you from up the trail I figured it was pretty safe."

"He'd kept me covered with his rifle since noon," the boy explained. "Guess he figured no one would be suspicious with me doin' that goddam hoein' there."

"What's your name, boy?" the stranger asked, sliding his gun back into the left-hand holster.

"Nathan Knight. My ol' man has the store over there." He pointed at the shacks, now warped silhouettes against the flaming sunset. He was aware of a smaller silhouette moving from them as his father, no doubt attracted by the gunfire, weaved towards them. "Drunken bum," the boy added.

The stranger made no comment, but removed his green-lensed glasses, and wiping them on his black silk kerchief, looked at Nathan with trail-inflamed eyes.

"Was you a-followin' this hombre?" asked Nathan. "Who was he?"

"I sure was," the stranger replied. "He left his cayuse dead back between the buttes. This is who he was." From the breast pocket of his soot-black shirt he took a handbill and unfolded it. Peering at it closely in the fading light, Nathan saw an artist's impression of the man who lay dead at their feet. Heavy type at the top of the bill announced:

5,000 DOLLARS REWARD
LORENZ SEGURO
WANTED FOR MURDER AND ROBBERY

The stranger bit back a curse, then slipped down into a sitting position. Nathan saw his left leg was glistening with blood seeping through the fabric of his trousers.

"You hurt bad, mister?"

"That first bullet got me," the stranger muttered between clenched teeth. His large handsome face had gone the colour of putty. "Didn't hurt me at first, now it's kinda caught up with me. Can you stop the bleedin'. . ."

Nathan knelt down and began to slit the sodden material. The bullet had left a neat puncture where it had entered the flesh just above the knee, and an equally neat hole where it had come out the other side. Blood was welling out of both wounds in time to the beating of the stranger's heart. He took the stranger's kerchief and, making it into a pad, set to work to stop the flow.

"You'd better get him back to the store."

Nathan looked up to see his father looming unsteadily above them. "Your Ma'll fix him all right."

"He'll be pretty heavy to carry," Nathan said. "Mebbe I'd better get the cart."

"Just let me lean on your shoulder an' I'll make it all right," the stranger gasped. "I bin shot worse'n this."

The boy struggled to help the big man to his feet, and he swayed when the stranger's arm fell heavily across his shoulders.

"Wha' 'bout him?" asked Nathan's father, pointing vaguely at the dead outlaw.

"Leave it for now..." muttered the stranger. "I'd be obliged if you could throw a tarpaulin over him... don't want the coyotes... got to get some signed evidence before we plant him . . ."

With the stranger dwarfing his helpers, the incongruous trio struggled over the rough ground to the ghost buildings of Red Buttes. When they arrived one of the windows in the general store had become a square of

8

yellow light from a kerosene lamp.

"Arabella, Arabella," roared Knight senior. "Rouse yourself, woman, a fella's been hurt."

The door opened and an angular woman, who looked as though the sun had burnt her out both physically and spiritually over the years, took charge. After the stranger had collapsed on Nathan's bed, the boy was sent off to capture his horse. He found it half an hour later in the heavy dusk, its reins caught in greasewood bush. After he had brought it back and cared for it, he entered the store and beheld his father in his usual position behind the counter with the usual bottle before him. But instead of the scowl which he normally wore, his face was animated. He held up the page of an old newspaper in an unsteady hand.

"We got an uncommon guest tonight, son," he slurred. "Yes, siree, quite … an … uncommon guest..."

He blinked at Nathan.

"It's all... about... him," he added, waving the paper. "Yes, siree, mighty ... uncommon ..."

"Aw, who the hell is he then?" Nathan demanded impatiently.

"Hannibal Reno," his father announced. "Hannibal... Reno ... himself."

"So who's Reno?"

"Recognised him right off. Soon as I… saw him. Read about him … in the paper … found it. . ."

Without a word Nathan walked over the creaking floor and plucked the paper from his father's hand. The headline proclaimed : "Dancer Brothers Captured by Reno."

"He some sort of sheriff?" Nathan demanded.

"Not ... him. He's jus' about ... the greatest bounty man ever was."

* * *

Nathan woke, and could smell the straw about him reminding him he was not in his own bed. That was occupied by a wounded stranger called Reno. The events of the previous afternoon returned to him vividly. Once more he saw the Colt Peacemaker fly in a graceful arc from the stranger's left hand to his right. Suddenly the boy was desperate to see him again. He struggled into his denims and was still buttoning his shirt as he ran from the outhouse to the back of the Red Buttes Provision and General Store.

"How's Reno, Ma?" he demanded, bursting into the kitchen. Mrs. Knight paused in the hymn she was singing and said: "He'll be all right, the Devil looks after his own. Let it be a lesson to you, Nathan. He is a violent man and he has suffered in consequence …"

"Yeah, but the other guy's dead," retorted the boy. "I wanna see him."

"I do not want you to talk to him," his mother snapped. "Such men corrupt

Nathan fled the kitchen and went round to the front of the store where his father, evil-tempered after his whisky bout, was cursing an old Indian who had come to haggle for nails and tobacco.

"Ain't you got no chores to do?" he snarled.

Nathan left the store and walked round the side of the building until he was opposite the window of his own room. By pressing his face against the glass he could see the still form of Reno on his bed. One arm hung down over the side of the bed so that the back of the stranger's hand rested on the floor. Close to it lay one of his blue-steel revolvers.

For a moment Nathan regarded the patient in silence, then he tapped the pane with his knuckle. The noise was not loud but its effect on the stranger was remarkable. The hand moved as though it had life of its own, reaching the gun and grasping it so that by the time Reno was upright the Peacemaker was ready cocked. He held it ready for action while his left hand burrowed under the pillow behind him until it emerged with the green-tinted spectacles which had surprised Nathan the evening before. Reno slipped them on deftly while the unwavering Colt remained pointed at the door.

"Mister Reno," Nathan called softly. The man looked up at the window, saw Nathan's squashed face and smiled faintly under his drooping moustache. He laid the gun down on the patchwork counterpane and beckoned the boy to come in.

Through the glass Nathan pointed in the direction of his parents and then shook his head. He made a pantomime of opening the window. Reno nodded. Painfully he swung his weight out of the bed and, leaning on the wall so that he would not have to put weight on his injured leg, managed to move far enough forward to slip the sash bolt.

As soon as the window was open Nathan squirmed through. Reno had got back into the bed, but the exertion had caused beads of sweat to run down his white features.

Nathan stood hesitantly in the middle of the floor, hardly knowing what to say to the big stranger who had impressed him so much the day before. His eyes wandered round the room, and fixed on the gun belt of black tooled leather that hung from a peg above the bed. It was the most beautiful piece of leatherwork Nathan had seen, and he knew it must have cost many dollars south of the border where only old Mexican craftsmen could make such things. Intricate patterns had been embossed on the holster's surface which was so fine it seemed to be wet when the light caught it. The silver buckles were in keeping with the fine design and wonderfully chased. Cartridges in the soft loops glittered

11

like gold in the morning light, and Nathan felt a strange tug at his heart. That gunbelt, so exquisite and yet so suitable to house the twin hone-handled instruments of death seemed to sum up everything about the stranger.

Laying back, Reno wiped the sweat from his face with a black kerchief.

"What can I do for you, son?"

"Sorry to trouble you when you ain't feelin' all that good," muttered the boy.

"That's okay. I'm glad to see you. If it hadn't been for you I guess I'd have been needin' a marker instead of just a-layin' here with a holed leg."

"I jus' wanted you to know your hoss was okay. I caught him last night an' I put carbolic on the place where the bullet had creased him."

Reno nodded. There was a pause. Nathan stared at his feet.

"There's just one thing I'd like to know, Mister Reno ..."

"Say on."

"That Mexican hombre you killed last night. Could you sorta tell me more about him."

A faint smile appeared under Reno's black moustache.

"Gimme water first," he muttered. "Your Ma made a good job of that leg, but today it feels like it's on fire."

Nathan sloshed water into a glass from a pitcher.

The wounded man gulped it gratefully, then said: "As far. as Lorenz is concerned there ain't more'n a mite to tell. I'd followed him up from Nogales. Nearly caught up with him at Bisbee, but he vamoosed just in time. I guess when he lost his cayuse he knew he'd have to stand an' fight."

"Was he your enemy?"

"Nope. But when the reward money reached

12

$5,000 I guessed it was time I went after him. I'm a bounty hunter... not a guy who has feuds."

Nathan nodded. "Yeah, I know. My Pa found an old bit of a paper with a picture of you on it. It must be a great life, trackin' down outlaws, livin' by your guns . . ."

Reno removed his green-tinted glasses and regarded the boy expressionlessly. For a while the silence was only broken by the drone of a fly.

"I ain't all that keen on talkin' about it," he remarked at last. "Specially as your Ma ..."

Nathan shrugged impatiently. "What she know about it?" he asked.

"Mighty little, I guess. But she's still your Ma. How old are you, boy?"

"Gettin' on for eighteen."

"An' what's eatin' you up inside?"

For a moment Nathan fought for words to describe his discontent, then muttered, "This goddam place."

"So why don't you quit? A strong fella like you could find a job somewheres there's a bit of life. Ever thought on bein' a puncher ... or mebbe a hunter?"

"Yeah, a hunter. I ain't bad with a rifle. I shot an eagle out of the sky once. I was up on one of them buttes."

"Must have been a good shot. What gun you got?"

"Aw, just an' ol' Springfield, the kind they used way back in the Mexican War. It was a smooth bore but I got a blacksmith to rifle it for me. That helped a lot. He paused and then said, "I couldn't get anythin' better, than workin' on this goddam patch in this goddam ghost town. I reckon I'd have quit, but it's them..." He jerked his thumb in the direction of the store's living room. "If I went I guess they'd starve to death. My ol'

13

man is always so full of rotgut he couldn't do the work... but it weren't always like that. I can remember him when I was small, puttin' up this place. He was full of fire then. I remember him sayin' this was gonna be the greatest trailside store in the territory, but the ore in the hills ran out quick an' the trail weren't used much no more. The folk began to quit, but Pa hung on, an' as things got worse he seemed to lose his steam.

"He became his own biggest customer for Old Vermont... an' the worse he got, the more Ma got religion. I guess he musta realised he hadn't the heart to start again. Now he trades with a few Injuns, and the odd drover that comes along the trail, but it ain't enough to keep 'em goin'."

Embarrassed at having talked so much, the boy fell quiet.

"Sounds tough," Reno remarked tonelessly.

"I guess I hate 'em most of the time," Nathan said suddenly. "But when I think of quittin' I feel kinda sorry. I usta have a kid sister but she got fever. It was after her death that things got real bad with 'em. Now Pa just rots his guts with whisky an' Ma sings hymns all day an' keeps tellin' him what a son-of-a-bitch he is."

Reno twisted in the bed and bit his lips as a stab of pain shot through his leg.

"Sorry, Mister Reno. I guess I shouldn't bother you now. I – I just wanted to tell you about your hoss ... I'll go."

The boy walked over to the door, opened it and then looked back at the big man.

"There's just one thing... I'm a good shot an' I ain't exactly a bad cook – I can knock up a meal when Pa's drunk an' Ma's havin' her visions – an' I'm used to hard work... well, I kinda wondered ... if I could ... if I could come along with you when you move on ..."

Reno turned his pain-twisted features to the boy, looked at him a moment and then, despite the spasm which was pressing his lips into a tight line, gave a short bark of laughter.

Nathan left the room, his eyes hot and dangerously close to tears.

CHAPTER TWO

"'To me belongeth vengeance and recompense ...'" quoted grey-haired Arabella Knight to her son. "That's what the Lord saith in Deuteronomy, and what the Lord saith in Deuteronomy is dead right. It ain't right for a man to do the Lord's work. Remember what happened when Gain killed his brother Abel? The Lord saith *'... whosoever slayeth Cain, vengeance shall be taken on him sevenfold. And the Lord set a mark upon Cain, lest any finding him should kill him.'"*

"Aw, that's Bible stuff," Nathan growled. "What's it gotta do with Hannibal Reno?"

"He has put hisself above the Lord," she retorted. "He hunts men down for vengeance, an' that makes him an evil varmint."

"He don't do it for vengeance – it's the reward. Anyways, if he's so goddam wicked, why d'you fix his wound like you do?"

"It ain't for me to judge a fellow sinnin' crittur," the boy's mother explained. "It's jest that I don't want no son of mine moonin' around wishin' he could be like him. An' don't try an' fool me you're not... I can read you easy as I can read the Good Book. Your father's bad enough influence, let alone professional slayers of men."

"Aw, let up, Ma."

"Well, you ain't to talk to him, an' if I catch you I'll get your Pa to tan ..."

Disgusted, the boy walked outside, his old Springfield under his arm. A week had passed since the gun battle at the maize patch, and Nathan knew that any day now Reno would mount his horse and ride back

16

along the trail that vanished between the red buttes. Several times he had tried to steer his conversation with Reno to his wish to go with him, but each time the bounty hunter had avoided it. Still, he would spend hours talking with the boy mostly about firearms which he knew fascinated him. Once he showed him how he had stripped down his single-action Colts and filed off the "dogs," leaving the trigger mechanism dead so he could fire by releasing the hammer with his thumb.

"Double-action guns are okay for those who don't have to shoot fast," he explained, "but if you are in a gun fight an' need speed you can lose a second while you try an' get your finger inside the guard an' on the trigger."

Such lore from an expert delighted Nathan, a fact that was promptly noted by his mother who did everything her scolding tongue could do to keep the two apart. When she tackled Reno about it he replied courteously. "Sure, I'll stop talkin' guns to the kid. I owe you a deep favour, ma'am, an' I wouldn't like to rile you none. It was jest that he seemed so interested, an' I figured he's kinda lonely ..."

Now Nathan was walking past the spot where Lorenz Seguro had met his end in the hail of Reno's bullets. All that remained of the drama was a small cross Reno had asked Nathan to nail together and put over the grave.

"Even a skunk like Seguro has the right of a marker," he'd said. Nathan felt it a waste of time, but had done it to please his idol. Prior to the burying of Seguro, Reno had got a paper signed testifying to his death and had asked Nathan to collect his weapons. The silver-plated pistol had a handsome monogram of LS engraved on the butt and it had brought a brief flicker of satisfaction to Reno's face.

"A lot of folk have seen that gun," he

remarked. "They'd know Lorenz would have to be dead to give it up."

Later on he'd remarked with a bleak smile: "Getting a guy can be tough, but it ain't as hard as claimin' the reward after ... Pat Garrett had to hire a lawyer and go to Sante Fe to get the State Legislature to pass a special act to collect the reward for shootin' Billy the Kid Bonney.

"Once I brought in a guy alive into a place called Paradise an' had him locked in the jail. Then I had to hang around. He was waitin' his trial an' I was waitin' for my money. One night, when it seemed I weren't likely to get it without a fight I sprung him. Two weeks later he came back an' robbed the Paradise bank an' shot down a couple of fellas. After that I've been paid pretty regular." It was about the only time Reno had mentioned anything in connection with his work, and then because he seemed to think it was a joke.

Leaving the rough cross, Nathan mooched along the trail along which Reno had ridden towards him in a halo of sunset. Soon Reno would be going back along the trail, leaving Nathan with his endless chores and loneliness which would be worse now that – through the bounty hunter – he had glimpsed a different and more exciting world, a world where a man could win freedom and fame by skill with his weapons.

Feeling thoroughly miserable, the boy looked about him with eyes bored by the scene that never changed – the desert stretching to the west where the horizon was so sharp it seemed that one could step over it and topple into infinity, the shimmering shacks of Red Buttes, and the towering rocks themselves. Suddenly he began walking towards the eastern one. In the past he had sometimes broken his lassitude by scaling its steep sides to the flat top

18

where he was a lonely monarch of all he surveyed. Today the danger and difficulty of the climb would take his mind off his discontent.

Half an hour later, with the Springfield slung across his back, he was toiling up the narrow track which wound up the lower part of the butte. Soon this dwindled to a ledge a few inches wide and after that Nathan had to heave himself up from handhold to handhold.

When he finally hauled himself over the edge at the top his shirt was dark with sweat. For some minutes he lay face down on the hot rock, his lungs labouring and his heart pounding painfully. At last he sat up, and with his rifle across his knees, viewed the world below. Once again he felt an old elation at having managed to make the ascent. He told himself that when he returned to the store he would see Reno and demand to go along with him. So far he had acted like a sulky kid – no wonder Reno had laughed. Now he'd prove to Reno that he was a man, and in a way that Reno would understand and appreciate. Why the hell hadn't he thought of it before!

From inside his pocket he brought out the folded newspaper page on which was printed Reno's portrait and a vivid description of how the bounty man had brought in the Dancer Brothers, a couple of rustlers who had killed a boundary rider and terrorised Cochise County until the price on their heads had risen enough to make Reno interested in their capture. When he had finally cornered them they had given in without a shot being exchanged.

Smoothing out the paper, Nathan began to spell out the story once more. He did it slowly because he had not had much schooling. He, with several other kids, had been taught his letters by the wife of a padre in the days when it seemed Red Buttes had a future. But when the inhabitants dwindled away, the padre and his family moved on to save souls in more prosperous areas. The Devil had very little interest in a ghost town. Since those distant days Nathan had had very little use for book learning.

Now he spelled his way through a description of the capture of the outlaws and their subsequent hanging. The eldest of the brothers had insisted on shaking hands with Reno before the noose was placed round his neck. The article ended: *"Most readers of this journal will have the usual prejudice against the bounty hunter who collects rewards in the same spirit as an Apache warrior collects scalps and whose very existence is paid for with blood money, yet the writer must point out that men like Hannibal Reno do have a place in contemporary society no matter how disagreeable the idea may be to other members of that society. The advantage of the bounty hunter in bringing malefactors to their rightful deserts is that he can take his own particular brand of law across state boundaries in pursuit of criminals and he cannot be subjected to political or other pressures. Finally he hunts only men who deserve punishment otherwise they would not have the prices on their heads which make them acceptable as game for the bounty man. In this way justice is served by the freelance."*

This last paragraph had little effect on Nathan and he did not bother to finish reading it. What had impressed him was the fact that Jim Dancer had wanted to shake Reno's hand. Sitting high above the world on top of the butte, the boy could imagine the scene... the sea of faces, the two men standing under the crossbar of the gallows, the marshal and a padre standing to one side and Hannibal Reno dressed in black walking up the steps to Jim Dancer.

It was said that young Tom Dancer expressed regret for his crime and had difficulty in holding back his tears of remorse, but not Jim. He wanted to be launched into eternity having shaken hands with the only man at the gathering he respected.

And then, with the two lifeless forms revolving slowly in the breeze, Nathan could imagine Reno swinging into his saddle and riding into the distance in search of some new quarry. To the boy the picture seemed so grand he realised why Reno had not wanted him. To Reno he was a "nothin' from nowhere," and yet, by God, he'd show Reno yet.

He stood up, the hot breeze ruffling the hair which hung over his eyes, and looked down at the dizzy earth below. There on the trail he saw a tiny, ant-sized figure in black, riding towards the ravine between the buttes.

It was Reno, and he was riding out on him, no doubt having timed his departure to please his Ma. Nathan felt sick as the gelding began to canter.

"You can't leave me," he yelled into the breeze which carried his words unheard across the wilderness. "If it hadn't bin for me you'd have been damn dead. You owe me somethin', an' you're sneakin' out, goddam you."

For a moment the black rider had disappeared from Nathan's view behind a shoulder of rock, but the boy knew that within seconds he would be in full sight again before he vanished a second time into the narrow defile between the two buttes.

He raised the Springfield. In a moment the backsight, the foresight and Reno would be in a deadly line. Nathan knew for a certainty that when he squeezed the trigger Reno would tumble dead from his horse. He felt it with the same clarity as when he'd aimed the rifle at an eagle, knowing that it would suddenly plummet out of the sky – and it had.

He had only to pull the trigger and for ever he would be known as "the man who had shot Hannibal Reno."

The bounty hunter appeared like a small black dot in the sights. "This is it, Reno," gritted the boy. Sweat sheened his forehead, his trigger finger began to tremble and his stomach knotted painfully. He tried to force .himself to squeeze the trigger, but it seemed as though he had suddenly become paralysed.

The Springfield fell with a clatter to the rock. Nathan buried his face in his hands and Hannibal Reno passed out of range into the deep shadow of the gorge. It was many hours before the boy was able to make the perilous descent of the east butte.

In the light of a candle Nathan Knight penned a letter to his sleeping parents, his tongue moving between his lips as he laboriously formed crude letters.

"Dere Pa and Ma," he had written. "This Letter wil tel you I have gone of at last as I have my Own Way to make and am sick to death of Red Buts. I am taking the mule and 9 Dolars and 55 Gents I found in the Store but will send this amount back as soon as I have earned Some Money plus other Money which I hope wil help you along."

Now he paused and chewed at his pencil until he bit the end right off. Inspiration did not come, so he tried to remember how he had been taught to end a letter by the padre's wife. Finally he wrote: "Yore obed, servant, N. Knight," and placed the paper on the counter against his father's half-emptied bottle of Old Vermont. "At least he'll find it soon enough," he murmured to himself.

A few minutes later he slipped out of the store,

saddled his father's skinny mule in the bright moonlight and then, with a roll of his few possessions on the pommel and the Springfield across his shoulders, he mounted and urged the reluctant animal along the trail towards the towering shapes of the red buttes.

* * *

A hot night held Gila City in its breathless grip. Nathan paused before the swinging doors of the Wheel of Fortune Saloon and Gaming Palace, drew a deep breath and pushed his way inside. After the dim streets of the sprawling frontier settlement, the brilliant light – magnified by huge chandeliers and rows of engraved mirrors – made him blink. The place was lit up like a stage set and full of men hell-bent on having a good time. Nathan gazed with an open mouth about him, bewildered by the assortment of frontier characters. On a small stage at the far end a line of girls danced a riotous version of the can-can; men, ranging from trail-thirsty punchers to slick frock-coated drummers lined the bar, bawling out the white-aproned barman. More sober groups sat round the gaming tables, faces expressionless and eyes hypnotised by their fans of cards as though the pasteboards held destiny's secrets. Nearby, miners sat round a large table singing in various raucous keys to the can-can tune, while a hostess laughed almost sincerely at their jokes and drank their champagne.

The pianist thumped out the final chord and leaned back mopping his face. A wild cheer rose from the spectators who had been crowding the stage, and one enthusiast unholstered his pistol, no doubt to express his appreciation by putting a bullet through the ceiling. But before he could get the weapon above his head a bouncer reached him, propelled him across the crowded floor and catapulted him out past Nathan into the dark Arizona night to an accompaniment of

23

jeers.

"Sorry, friend," the bouncer cried as the unfortunate sprawled in the dust by the hitching rail, "but Fortune spent too many dollars on them chandeliers for doggoned varmints like you to shoot up."

Inside the pianist gulped a schooner of beer and struck up. The dancers – glittering in sequins and silvered feathers – began their next number with smiles for all and special winks for those who seemed to be happy spenders.

The light, the shouting, the music and the girls overwhelmed Nathan so that for a sickening moment he wished he was back in the dreary familiarity of Red Buttes.

He had arrived at Gila City at sundown, three days after running away from home. This was the first large settlement on the trail and here he hoped to get news of Reno. He had walked the boardwalk of Silver Street, his eyes greedy as he gazed at the people who made up the lively town. There were dusty cattlemen mincing along in their high-heeled riding boots; dirt-streaked miners in to sell their ore, teamsters with coiled bull-whackers, a gang of buffalo hunters, their clothes stiff with dried blood, and a be-whiskered prospector or two escaping from the desert for a spree.

After his solitary life at Red Buttes, Nathan felt bewildered by Gila City. Until darkness fell he had wandered the dusty streets determinedly in the hope of seeing the tall black form of Reno limping along. He even knocked at the door of a rooming house, and at a building which had blazoned across its false front "Gila City Palace Hotel," but at both places the clerks shook their heads without interest when he asked if they knew a certain Hannibal Reno.

Now the purple night had fallen on the town, he was determined to search the night spots to find

24

Reno. And as he stood by the doors his eyes, now accustomed to the colourful glare, searched for the man who had come to have such a fascination for him.

"You gonna stand there all night, fella?" demanded the bouncer after he had watched the customer he had just ejected crawl away. "You're kinda blockin' the trail. This here place is for gents to drink, not a free sideshow for outback bums."

At his words someone nearby sniggered. Nathan felt the blood rush to his face. Compared with this well-dressed throng he must certainly look ridiculous in his patched denims and working shirt.

"He's mebbe a survivor from Bull Run," said a wag, pointing at the ancient Springfield Nathan held in his left hand.

Ill at ease, the boy walked from the door and found himself a place at the end of the bar.

"What'll it be, fella – sarsaparilla or buttermilk?" joked a barman, running his fingers along his huge moist moustache with satisfaction at his shaft of wit.

"Rye," Nathan murmured, laying his beloved rifle against the wall at the corner of the bar where he hoped it would be unnoticed.

With a practised flick of the wrist the barman spun a glass to the boy who only just managed to grab it before it fell off the handsome mahogany counter. The whisky was poured and – to Nathan's relief – the man with the apron left to serve a noisy group of patrons calling loudly for beer.

Turning his back to the bar, Nathan continued to absorb the interior of the Wheel of Fortune. For once in his life he felt like agreeing with his mother; she had always described saloons to him as "halls of Satan."

After another drink he felt better. They could laugh at him now, but once he was with Reno it would be another story ...

"There's a funny kinda smell round here," a voice said close to him.

"Sure is," replied a second. "Puts me in mind of a barn that has had beeves in it."

"Could be," agreed the first. "Sure is a farm smell, but it reminds me more of hawgs ..."

"Or mebbe a skunk ..."

This time instead of flushing, Nathan's face went dead white. He turned to the two tall punchers standing beside him.

"What'd ya mean?" he muttered thickly.

"No offence, stranger," laughed the taller of the two, winking at his mate. "It's jus' that me an' my pard thought we could smell somethin' which kinda reminded us of somethin'..."

"Hawgs," interrupted the second man.

"Yeah, hawgs, or mebbe a skunk. You don't happen to be in the hawg line of business do you, friend?"

"Or mebbe you are a skunk herder ... ?"

Nathan's fists knotted. He stepped back giddily, his arm going back ready to land a blow at his tormentors. Before his fist could piston forward, fingers of steel gripped his wrist. He turned his head to see the moustached barkeep who held his arm locked in his hands.

"Don't do that, friend," the man said calmly. "Fortune likes her place peaceful..."

"I don't give a goddam what Fortune likes, or who the hell Fortune is ..." exploded the boy, close to tears of rage.

"That's a pity," came a cool feminine voice from his left. "I guess it's easy to see your manners are out of the same stable as your clothes."

Nathan's head snapped round from the barman

to the owner of the soft voice. He saw a young woman regarding him with cool grey eyes. Immediately he forgot the two cattlemen who had been mocking him. He was stunned at the sight of the woman. Unlike the other female habituees of the saloon, she was almost primly dressed in a long gown of some midnight blue material. At the cuffs and collar there were small splashes of lace, and he noticed that on her slender hands she wore a number of rings scintillating in the light. Her face was oval, with a flawless olive complexion, while her hair, as black and gleaming like oiled ebony, framed her face and fell in two cascades to the generous swell of her breast. She was tall, almost as tall as the tongue-tied boy, and when she walked he was not surprised to see that she moved with the same dangerous grace that he had once seen in a cougar back at Red Buttes.

"I am Fortune Sarrat," she continued. "I own this place..." She raised her hand and Nathan's mouth gaped again as he saw her place a long, thin cheroot between her lips. She smiled at his obvious surprise. "And I'm also the slickest gambler in these parts," she added with a touch of pride. "How come you ain't heard of me?"

"I – I'm sorry, ma'am," mumbled Nathan. "I guess I didn't mean no disrespect. I was sort of riled up cause these *hombres* were ..."

She nodded.

"Come and buy me a drink," she said. "Bring the rye over, Pete," she ordered the barkeep.

"Right away, Miss Fortune, ma'am," he replied, stooping under the bar flap with sudden agility. Obviously her word was law in the Wheel of Fortune.

The girl found a small table in a corner and sat down, her back to the wall. Her eyes moved restlessly round the large hall while she inhaled cigar smoke.

27

Nathan sat opposite her, his mind still in a whirl at the turn of events.

Pete placed the bottle on the table and stood meaningfully by the boy. Nathan put his hand in his hip pocket and handed the barman all the coins he had without any idea of how much he was expected to pay. Contemptuously, the barman gave him some back and left.

"Here's to fortune," said the girl, raising her glass. "What are you doin' in my place? You look like you belong back on the old homestead."

"Looks ain't everything" he muttered.

"You quit the old homestead then? You run off an' left your Ma and Pa to get on hoeing the bean patch?"

He nodded.

"Was that the last of your money – that what you gave Pete?"

"Yeah, I didn't bring much... ain't much there to bring from where I come from."

"Okay," she said, as though dismissing him. "Come round tomorrow – not too early – an' you can have a handout. Just enough to get some clothes and get you started. When you make your pile, come back an' lose it at my tables."

"Lady," Nathan said, "I ain't lookin' for no handout. I know you mean it kindly, but keep your charity for them as can't look after theirselves."

Her eyes flicked back to him.

"Proud!"

"I don't know, ma'am, but I know I ain't a bum yet."

"Good lad," she smiled slightly, showing a row of slightly pointed teeth which gleamed white in contrast with her olive skin and dark lips. "Have a drink. What's your name?"

"Nathan Knight. I've come up the trail from Red Buttes. I'm lookin' for a fella ... mebbe you've heard tell of him. He's ..."

He saw that her gaze had turned from him and she was looking at a man who was approaching their table. A strange, ironic expression played round her mobile mouth.

Nathan saw he was of medium height, fresh complexioned with bright blue eyes, curly fair hair and a neat pointed beard. He was obviously a dandy, and over his spotless white shirt wore a waistcoat of brocade. Like many of the men in the Wheel of Fortune he wore a gun with the holster secured to his thigh with a thong to prevent it riding up.

"Hey, Fortune," he began loudly, "I want a few words with you ... and not in front of this hick."

"That isn't the way for a gen'l'man to address a lady," Fortune said softly. "I'm boss of this outfit, and don't you forget it, Charley Donohue. Now get back to the faro table an' I'll talk to you later ..."

"You weren't talkin' to me like that last night, you bitch," he snarled.

Suddenly Nathan found himself on his feet. Without thought, and with an ease which seemed to come to him naturally, his fist swept in an arc and crunched against the jaw of the dandy. For a moment the man swayed, his blue eyes glaring and the breath whistling through his nostrils.

"You've asked for what you're gonna get, stranger," he hissed. Nathan found himself looking down into the muzzle of Donohue's Smith and Wesson.

29

CHAPTER THREE

At the sound of the blow Nathan had landed on Donohue's face, the patrons of the Wheel of Fortune dropped their voices and raised their eyes from the cards. On the small stage the can-can girls forgot their dance routine as they stood on their toes, craning to get a better view. The only person who did not seem to notice the drama immediately was the piano player who continued to thump several honky-tonk bars before he too felt the air of hushed excitement which had fallen over the assembly. Raising his eyes from the keys, he saw the tableau of the dandified Donohue pointing his gun at the belly of the uncouth stranger. His fingers became still.

Nathan stood tense and silent as the man with the gun eyed him up and down. He had no idea of what was going on around him. Instinct told him that he must not take his eyes off the face of Donohue who, merely by contracting the muscles of his forefinger, could snuff him out like a candle. When he had been covered by the Mexican's rifle in the maize patch, Nathan had felt little fear. It had been too impersonal. He had merely been an accidental factor, but now it was different. He had struck this man, hurting his pride as well as his face. The expression in his eyes told Nathan that he was going to make sure of getting his revenge. The boy's stomach knotted in almost physical pain at the anticipation of a bullet from the Smith and Wesson. Yet there was still room in his emotions for a slight quirk of satisfaction as he saw flesh purpling from the blow of his fist.

"I reckon you feel kinda safe, havin' hit

me," Donohue drawled dangerously. "Guess you thought as you weren't wearin' an iron you could get away with throwin' a punch at me. Was you tryin' to prove somethin' to that *lady* by hittin' me? Was you earnin' your handout, pal?"

Nathan said nothing. Behind him several men had begun to grin wolfishly. They had seen Goodtime Charley Donohue in action before.

"Anyways, pal, I can see you ain't used to society. I guess manners an' deportment ain't rated that high on the bean patch where you comes from, so I'm gonna teach you. Firstly, pal, you don't ever butt into other folks' business 'cause when you do, this is what happens ..."

With the speed of a striking snake the man's left hand swung and cracked across Nathan's face. The boy fell back, his eyes watering and his head dizzy. Calmly Donohue stepped forward and swung his hand back and forwards. The noise of the blows, rather like a series of hand claps, echoed through the Wheel of Fortune. Blood dribbled from Nathan's battered lips, then began to flow from his nostrils.

Through the red haze that was forming about him, Nathan was vaguely aware of someone calling out, a woman's voice telling Donohue to stop. But the to-and-fro of the hard hand continued, and he continued to stagger back, back towards the corner of the bar where his despised Springfield was hidden in the shadow.

At last, when the lower half of his face was a bloody mask, Donohue dropped his arm. He was panting with his effort, and the tip of his tongue slid along the edge of his sharp teeth in sadistic satisfaction.

"Now I'm gonna teach you somethin' else, pal. Dancin' leads to great social success ... so, dance, pal, dance." :

The barrel of the revolver tilted down. Donohue

fired and a bullet splintered the floor between Nathan's clumsy boots. He leapt back. There was a hoot of laughter. Having hurt him, Donohue was now going to ridicule him. The second bullet actually nicked a piece out of the toe of the boot. There was a slight sensation of pain, but the victim was hardly aware of it. What was more important was that he could feel his back against the edge of the bar. He began to cower away from his tormentor, shuffling to the left with his rump muscles taut against the mahogany.

"Jump," commanded Donohue. Nathan jumped. It was lucky for him or his foot would have been smashed by the .32 bullet.

Will he use up all his shells? Nathan wondered, continuing to edge along the long bar. To the onlookers it appeared as though he was merely trying to escape towards the door,

A voice slurred, "That's enough, Donohue. You paid him up, let him go." It was an old prospector who had been steadily drinking his way through a tiny bag of nuggets he had brought in from the desert.

Charley Donohue ignored him, and the several cries of "Grandpa's right," "Jus' throw him out," and "Cool off, Donohue."

"Hear that, pal," Donohue hissed. "You got friends. There's always someone that feels kindly for a whupped cur. Now you apologise to me, an' I'll mebbe take their advice. I'll just kick you into the street an' give you an hour to vamoose. Jus' say: 'Sorry, Mister Donohue.' "

Nathan shook his head. The gun exploded, and there was some laughter as Nathan sprang back by reflex action.

"A pity you wasn't wearin' of a gun," Donohue said through the powder smoke which curled about him. "It would have saved you this – you'd have been peacefully dead by now."

Nathan continued to slide himself along the bar and his elbow knocked a bottle which crashed to the floor.

"Beg my pardon an' you can go."

Again he shook his head, not trusting himself to speak. He continued to sidle towards the end of the bar, his left hand outstretched for the Springfield propped in the shadow where the bar joined the wall. Any moment now and his hand would close on the cold metal of the barrel. As he moved like one in mortal fear, he watched Donohue closely from between his swollen eyelids.

The gunman no longer pointed the pistol at him. It was obvious to him that there was no fight in the boy.

Any moment now, thought Nathan. Gawd, jus' let me get my hands on that gun . . .

Suddenly a girl yelled shrilly: "Look out, Charley, there's a gun..."

Spitting out a curse, Nathan turned. But before he could locate his weapon something seemed to explode in his head. A wave of utter darkness swept over him, his knees buckled and he collapsed on the sawdust-strewn floor.

"It's okay, fella, you ain't on your way to Boothill yet."

Painfully Nathan opened his eyes, blinked at the blinding light of morning, and tried to establish where he was. The pain in his head made him giddy even though he was laying full length on some narrow bed. His face was puffy – his lips alone must be swollen to twice their normal size. His hand stole up to his mouth, his fingers checking to see if he had lost any teeth.

"Doc Williams says you ain't got a busted head so you'll be all right in a while. Better a headache than a bullet through your guts."

Nathan moved his head slightly and the world seemed to capsize. Close to his face he could see a metal rod running vertically. By squinting he could make out another and another.

"Afore you ask me where you are," continued the dry voice, "I'll tell you – you are in the Gila jailhouse, havin' been arrested for disturbin' the peace."

A moan escaped from Nathan's clenched teeth.

"Gawd a'mighty, I feel sick," he muttered.

"Guess you do. Goodtime Charley treated you tough, an' when I had to pistol whip you it didn't help none. Here, drink this."

A pannikin of water was pushed between the bars of the cell. By making a fantastic effort Nathan was able to raise his head and guide the tin to his lips. He sucked the water down greedily.

"Thanks, mister, whoever you are," he muttered when his head dropped back to the corn shuck palliasse.

"I'm Matt Hollis, and I'm Town Marshal here."

Nathan made another attempt at opening his eyes and turning his head. Beyond the bars he saw the marshal, a man with carroty hair, a red stubble and a large, bulky body which, for all its size, moved with surprising ease.

"I went into the Wheel of Fortune last night when I heard the shootin'," he explained. "I managed to take a swipe at you just before Donohue put a bullet in you. You could never have got that rifle up in time. Afterwards, Fortune wanted you arrested …"

"I didn't do no harm to her surely?"

"'Course not. But she knew that this was one place where you'd be safe from Donohue. She also got the Doc to come and look at you. In her way she was quite concerned. I gather you sorta stuck up for her."

There was silence. Hollis lolled behind his battered desk, grinning with good humour at his battered prisoner.

"Who is Donohue, anyways?" murmured Nathan at last.

"A gunman… certainly not the sort of fella for the likes of you to punch. For some months he's been employed by Fortune at the Wheel of Fortune. Y'know, dealin' cards, takin' a hand at faro, makin' sure there ain't no cheatin', showing off his gun in case of trouble. When a girl runs a gambling saloon, she needs a guy like Donohue around. But she's fired him now. They've had a big bust up. I sorta got the impression he was aimin' to take over the Wheel."

The marshal began to fill a pipe. "If you feel like any breakfast, I'll get some sent over from Li Chong's."

Nathan felt a wave of sickness at the thought of food.

"What's gonna happen to me now?" he asked.

"Waal, you'll be tried an' if you're found guilty for disturbin' the peace, you'll be fined and then run outa town. In fact so you won't break no more peace I'll have you put on the stage~ I guess Fortune is scairt that Donohue or his friends will shoot you now that he's lost his job."

Nathan heard a door open and close.

"Hello, Eddie. He's woke up. The court is

35

just about to sit."

Nathan saw a tall man, with a long sad face and grizzled hair, holding a coffee pot. Its smell filled the small jail.

"Eddie's my deputy," said Matt Hollis in his genial way. "He looks sour as hell but you ought to hear him on his old bull fiddle . . ."

"Want some coffee, prisoner?" asked Eddie in a deep melancholy voice.

"I'll sure try some."

"An' we'll get the court business over," said the marshal. "Knight – that's your name, ain't it? – you are accused of breakin' the peace by causin' a ruckus in the Wheel of Fortune saloon. Guilty or not guilty?"

"I dunno."

"You hit Donohue, didn't you?"

"Guilty."

"Good boy. It's the decision of this court to impose a fine of ten dollars."

He paused and swallowed some coffee with noisy 'satisfaction.

"You got ten dollars?"

"Nope."

"Eddie, go an' sell his mule ... unless you'd rather that old Springfield was sold?"

"Keep me the gun," Nathan said. He drank some coffee and. then went back to sleep. For a while Matt Hollis looked at his form on the prison bunk curiously, then shook his head;

"Fancy gettin' beat up like that over a woman."

It was afternoon when Nathan woke. Though his head still ached, he felt much better than when he had first come to in the cell.

"Eddie got eleven dollars fifty for your mule," said the marshal. "I guess he shoulda been a hoss trader. Here's the money."

He pushed a bundle of notes through the bars.

"Now, gimme ten an' I'll be able to release you when the next stage leaves Gila." Mechanically Nathan handed back ten singles. Hollis counted them, put five into a drawer of his desk and five into his hip pocket.

"The marshal gets half of all fines," he explained.

"That makes you a regular bounty hunter," Nathan said with the trace of a grin.

"Don't try an' be funny. I take my money fair an' legal as an elected representative of the law... I ain't got no time for them bounty huntin' sons-of-bitches. They don't keep the law, they just want blood money like goddam leeches. Why, I'd rather have an honest badman any day than deal with them human vultures."

"I knew one once," said Nathan, trying to sound off-handed, "He seemed sorta special."

"Any guy with a gun is sorta special," the marshal retorted. He was about to say more when a man in a dark suit entered carrying a small leather bag.

"Hi, Doc, come to see the prisoner?"

He nodded.

"Fortune wanted me to check you're all right," he said to Nathan. "Feeling any better?"

"I feel like a herd of beeves stampeded right over me," Nathan replied. "That Donohue plays it rough. I'd sure like to meet him again when my head stops goin' round ..."

"That's no way to think," Matt Hollis grunted while the doctor entered the cell and began looking at the bruise across the back of Nathan's neck where the marshal had hit him with the long barrel of his Navy Colt.

37

"What chance do you think you'd have against a guy like Goodtime Charley Donohue?" Hollis continued. "He's a professional killin' machine. They reckon he downed at least ten fellas in fair shoot-outs. No, fella, you're gonna hit the trail out of Gila an' live to tell the tale. Them's Fortune's orders."

"Tell me about this Fortune," Nathan said.

"Well, Fortune is ... she's kinda ... well, she ain't... aw hell, you tell him, Doc."

"She's a very remarkable young woman," Doctor Williams, said gravely. "She's the only woman gambler I have ever met. I understand she gambles very skilfully, that is how she got the money to start the Wheel of Fortune. She can certainly hold her own with men, though some think she is too hard for a woman, but I happen to know that she has done various acts of kindness ..."

"Yeah," Nathan agreed, sitting up on the plank bunk. "She's even offered me a handout. Say, Doc, could you look at my foot. It's kinda painin'..."

The doctor looked down at the heavy farm boot with the piece shot out of the toe. Without a word he cut through the leather laces and eased it off, Nathan wincing as he did so.

"Uh-huh," said the doctor. Nathan saw that his sock was saturated with blood. "He's taken off half of your little toe," Doctor Williams explained. "You'll find walkin' a mite hard for a while. I'll clean it up." He opened his bag and set to work. Nathan said nothing, but Matt Hollis noticed that his swollen lips had settled into a grim line which gave the Marshal cause for reflection.

* * *

The next day Marshal Hollis and Eddie escorted a limping Nathan down to the stage office. The two men were on the alert for trouble, but it was early morning and, apart from a small group standing round the Concord coach, the streets were deserted. Here and there pencil lines of smoke rose from the shacks into the still, watercolour blue of the sky, but it seemed that most of the inhabitants of Gila were sleeping off the night before. Only out at the mines had the day's work started.

Matt Hollis nodded to the stage driver who was standing at the head of his team of six horses, his coiled rawhide under his arm. Eddie loaded Nathan's roll and the Springfield on the top of the coach.

"This is the gent," said the marshal. "I don't want him off this coach until you hit Silver Springs. I guess he should have cooled his blood by then."

Just as Nathan was about to be ushered in, an old negro shambled up to him and held out an envelope.

"Mis', Fortune, she done send you this," he mumbled.

Nathan pocketed it and took his place in the Concord coach. There were only five other people in it, a couple of smart-suited drummers with sample cases at their feet, a tall cattleman and a pretty girl who was travelling with an older, sour-looking woman who was obviously her aunt.

"Good luck, fella," said the marshal, and slammed the door. The other passengers looked hard at Nathan. With his battered face and stained clothes he looked even less prepossessing than when he had first ridden into Gila. The aunt sniffed loudly to express her disgust at having to travel with such a savage.

Outside the shotgun guard climbed up next to the driver. The whip pistol-cracked, harness creaked and, rocking gently on its leather thorough braces, the coach began to roll out of Gila City.

No one spoke.

Nathan tore open the envelope the Negro had handed him. In it was 50 dollars in notes and a piece of paper on which was written simply: *"Knight by nature as well as name – thank you. Fortune"*

He thrust the money into his pocket. So Fortune had given him a handout after all. He grinned painfully. That handout was going to be mighty useful.

The coach, its paint and varnish gleaming, was now swaying speedily along the open trail. From his corner seat Nathan gazed through the window. Outside the ground looked hard and rocky. He did not want to land on that. If he waited sooner or later the Concord would have to slow down and he could seize his chance. Yet every minute he was moving farther and farther away from Gila.

At length the horses began to labour up a steep incline, and as the stage slowed Nathan leaned forward and opened the door of the coach. He heard a Babel of protest which was cut short abruptly as he flung himself out. He hit the edge of the trail with a thump that knocked the wind from his body, and rolled over and down the steep side of the slope to a dry arroyo. He came to rest in a patch of thorny chaparral and lay for a minute staring at the startlingly blue sky above.

The squeal of the Concord's brakes floated to him from a distance, followed by several excited voices trying to explain to the driver what had happened. His reaction was the expert utterance of a fluent string of cusswords.

Above the profanity came the high, knife-edged voice of the aunt: "I shall complain to the company. Fancy letting a dangerous prisoner travel with decent honest folks."

"He weren't no goshdarned prisoner," the driver retorted. "Matt Hollis jest wanted him out of town for his own good. Still, I figure if he wants to quit the coach, it ain't our problem. I can't see no sign of him ... can you, Dave?"

"My bet says he's down in that arroyo," the shotgun guard replied. "I guess Matt'll be as mad as a steer with itch if we don't find him ..."

"Yeah, an' the company won't exactly award us medals if we lost time."

"Perhaps he's hurt," came the voice of the girl. "While you're just talking he might be laying injured... or dying even."

"Victoria, Victoria, that is no way for a lady to behave," screeched the aunt a moment later. Shifting his gaze slightly, Nathan saw through the parched foliage that the girl from the coach was making her way down the slope. Obviously she was more headstrong than he had thought possible from seeing her sitting demurely opposite her aunt. He tried to worm his way into the shade of a large rock which hid him from the passengers who were now standing on the edge of the trail, watching the girl's erratic descent.

There was a crackling of chaparral. Nathan saw the merry, fair complexioned face of Victoria framed in long golden tresses.

Seeing him she did not start, but just mouthed: "Are you all right?" He nodded, and she moved on along the gulch.

"Come back, Victoria, there may be snakes there," the aunt commanded.

"D'ya see any sign of that bum, miss?" the exasperated driver asked.

"Only some broken branches where he fell," she shouted back. "He can't be hurt anyway."

41

"All right, so long as he ain't layin' there with a busted leg let's raise dust." A minute later the cracking of rawhide told Nathan the coach had resumed its uphill journey.

He picked himself up, tried to brush the hair out of his eyes and then began to limp back towards Gila. It was noon when he reached the outskirts of the town. As he drew nearer he had left the trail and had begun to approach it from open country.

Soon he was walking along one of the outer streets. A couple of loungers looked at him curiously from the deep shade of verandahs, but neither spoke. At the end of the street he turned into a small shack which bore a gunsmith's sign over the door.

In the gloom within Nathan was conscious of racks of rifles screwed to the wall, a chain thoughtfully placed through their trigger guards, and cases of gleaming pistols. Behind the counter lounged a fleshy, smooth-faced man – obviously new from the East by the way he spoke – who looked up as Nathan limped in, with a salesman's smile sliding into place on his features.

"Yes, sir, and what can I do for you?" he beamed. "Looking for a good all-round farm gun. A shot gun perhaps..."

Nathan looked at him bleakly.

"It ain't for no shotgun for no farm," he murmured. "I wanna six-gun for me."

"Of course, sir, of course," said the salesman hastily. "We have a nice line in Colts and Smith and Wessons . . . and a few imported guns. A gent like you might be interested in this foreign model. It has several unique features, including a knife that folds back under the barrel. Very handy in some circumstances I'm told."

"I know what I want," said Nathan. "I wanna second hand Colt Peacemaker, a good gun that's been run in with care, an' a holster that was made to take it."

The man nodded and pulled out a drawer.

"Here's an Army model," he said, holding up a revolver in a brown holster. "Nice walnut butt. Belonged to a fella had an argument with Charley Donohue, it's nicely balanced."

"Nope – it might be a hexed gun. I wanna lucky gun."

"Hmm," the salesman sighed. "I ain't ever heard of a lucky gun. I think all guns are bad luck sooner'or later for somebody." He dragged more weapons out of a drawer. "How do you like this, sir, I'm sure it's a lucky gun. It's got an eagle carved on the butt..."

Nathan felt it, frowned and said: "Don't feel balanced right to me."

"You must know a lot about guns."

"Nope, ain't never had nothin' but an old Springfield... but any fool can tell if a handgun feels right. Lemme try that one."

"Ah, yes, this one is rather special," said the man. "Nice ivory butt... lovely finish on the steel, and the mechanism is perfect." He clicked the cylinder and the clicking sounded crisp and satisfactory to Nathan's ear. Perhaps it was merely the white butt which reminded him of the Colts worn by Hannibal Reno, but as soon as his hand closed on the cool bone he knew that this was the gun he wanted.

"It's got a nice belt and holster," the salesman purred. "Supple leather..."

"Okay, I'll take it," said Nathan, drawing out the money which he had received from the owner of the Wheel of Fortune. He began peeling off notes.

"Excuse me asking," said the man, relaxed now that he had made a sale, "but aren't you the fella ...?"

"Probably," Nathan replied, strapping on the heavy black belt and adjusting it to suit him. "I'll want some boxes of ammunition. I've gotta learn how to work this goddam thing."

The salesman counted out the money, smiled his well-oiled smile and bid Nathan good morning. He had forgotten to add that the last owner of the bone-handled Colt was now occupying the latest grave in the cemetery just outside the town.

Nathan Knight left Gila City and limped along the vague trail which wound out to Boothill. His foot was hurting where Charley Donohue's bullet had smashed his small toe, and the unusual weight of the gun on his thigh did not help matters. He knew that, apart from when a funeral was taking place and most of Gila turned out for the occasion, this area was usually deserted.

He climbed the low hill and followed the trail over its brow where a collection of gravestones and wooden markers straggled in uneven ranks within the enclosure of an unpainted paling fence. As he looked at the pathetic burial ground, he felt a strange sadness. The chances were that within a few hours his body might be lowered into a shallow grave here. No more would he be able to look up at the blue sky above, no more be able to feel the hot desert wind on his face, not even curse the monotonous work which he had hated so much. He would be dead for ever, his life evaporated like water spilt on sand, and he might never have lived at all. And if he did not end up here, Charles Donohue, professional gunman and bully, would. His life would be ended, and all the meanness which he had practised during it would be just as meaningless to him as it had been to others during his lifetime.

The pointlessness of it suddenly overwhelmed the boy. Until that moment his life had been straightforward, his greatest ambition had been to escape from Red Buttes and own a rifle he could be proud of. Now he was. caught up in a destiny he could not even begin to understand. Yet he knew that he could not stop now. Before sunset he must confront Donohue and wipe out the shame which the gunslinger had planted in him.

He wished he had the coolness of Hannibal Reno – and his skill with firearms. Entering the enclosure, he stood in the shade of a Joshua tree and made an attempt to draw the revolver. His hand hit the butt, his fingers closed on the cool bone and he tried to snatch the gun from the holster. As he did so, the fore-sight caught the leather and the holster rode up with the gun.

"Goddam it to hell," he murmured, a fine sweat breaking out on, his face. He was filled with a sickly panic. Donohue would have had time to empty his gun into him while he had struggled with his holster. He only had a few hours to master the Colt. He had the feeling that Death was behind him, watching his efforts with sardonic amusement. The picture of the bloodied body of Lorenz Seguro flashed before his eyes ...

He endeavoured to adjust the holster but it made little difference. He was not even accustomed to the weight of the weapon, and even when he managed to withdraw it, the gun came away at an awkward angle.

At last he abandoned the fruitless practice with the Peacemaker and turned his attention to firing it. He raised it at arm's length and aimed at a small barrel cactus about thirty feet away. Cautiously his finger tightened on the trigger until the hammer fell on the cap. The gun exploded and a furrow appeared some distance from the cactus. But what worried the boy most was the way the gun bucked as he fired. He was beginning to realise the world of difference between a handgun and a rifle.

45

He fired some more rounds, then returned to the job of drawing.

"Are you aiming on committing suicide?" came a cool voice from behind him. He spun round, gun in hand, and saw Fortune sitting side-saddle on a grey mare on the other side of the picket fence. He lowered the gun, but kept his pale blue eyes on her face. She had a contemptuous expression on her full lips.

"I went to some trouble to get you out of town safe," she said, flicking her quirt impatiently. "Now you've come back to play a damn fool hero. You'll be dead by sundown the way you're going."

He wiped his swollen lips on the back of his hand, but said nothing.

"I've been watching you with that gun," Fortune continued. "Funniest thing I've seen in a mighty long time. If you go after Donohue like that, he'll probably die laughing... Now, listen, Knight. Take my horse and get out while you're still alive. The word has gone round Gila that you have bought a gun, and if you show up there again Donohue will drop you on sight. He blames you for the fact that he is no longer at the Wheel."

Still Nathan did not speak. For a while the two looked at each other. The only sound was the sigh of the breeze in the Joshua tree and the faint rattle of crucifixion thorn.

"Oh, why did you have to come back, you dumb loco ox," the girl cried impatiently.

"If I was an Injun, I'd say it was written," said Nathan softly. "Donohue made me a fool in front of all them folk. I guess that didn't matter too much, they was already thinkin' I was somethin' pretty funny. But he did it in front of you, too, and I have to even that up. To you I seemed like some stumble-bum who couldn't look after himself, who had to be

46

grubstaked and helped. I've just got to show you that ain't so..."

A strange expression crossed Fortune's olive features.

"And you think that by fighting Donohue that's going to prove something to me," she said. "Do you know what it will prove ... it'd prove that you are a pistolero like him. Besides, you don't stand a bat's chance in hell with Charley. He was using a pistol before he cut his teeth."

"That's as maybe," muttered Nathan. "At least it'll also prove that I ain't yeller, it'll prove that I don't need to shelter behind your skirts, beggin' your pardon. Mebbe he's better than me at gun-fightin', but once I can get the gun out I reckon I'm pretty straight. I've a good eye. I know that because of my old Springfield. Why, I once shot an eagle out of the sky..."

Fortune shrugged impatiently, then slid to the ground, She looped the reins round a paling and then entered the enclosure.

"You sure pick the dandiest place to practise in," she remarked drily. "Now, when I was watching you try to draw, I saw how the muzzle of the gun kept hitting the rim of your holster. If you have a clasp knife we'll cut away the leather to give it free passage. I guess the man who had this before you was quite a bit taller... And if you take one of your bootlaces and tie the bottom of the holster to your thigh it won't ride up. Come on, I'll show you ..."

CHAPTER FOUR

Charley Donohue sat before his glass at a table in Muller's Beer Garden. The garden was in fact a plot of dirt beside a grog shop. It had a few shady trees under which Muller's patrons killed their thirsts at rickety tables. Its great advantage was that it was situated on a slight rise at the edge of Gila City and therefore caught any breeze which blew across the plains. Now, in the late afternoon, the warm, restless air was stirring the leaves of the trees above the heads of Donohue and his half-dozen friends.

"I still bet you he won't show," a wispy man called Coleman was saying. "Even a hick like that must know an ace-high gunfighter when he sees one! – you sure taught him who was boss in the Wheel."

Donohue looked at him with a slight expression of contempt, but the jackal is complementary to the lion and Donohue did not object to having hangers-on. He waved his hand to the door of the shanty where fat Muller was picking his teeth and dreaming of the old country to which he would return once he had made his fortune out of these Western barbarians.

"Coming, Herr Donohue," he answered, and soon fresh glasses were placed on the table before the party.

"You heard any more about that kid that came back off the stage?" asked Donohue casually.

"Nein, Herr Donohue," replied the Beer Garden proprietor. "I chust heard he vas buying a shooter this morning."

"I'd like to eat," Donohue announced. "How about a thick steak, Muller."

"Ya, a nice steak. I vill get Gretchen cooking

steaks for you and the boys."

Donohue and his friends leaned back in their chairs. From the beer garden they had a fine view of the plain unrolling itself to the ragged horizon. The breeze was pleasant, and at any other time Charley Donohue would have been at peace with the world.

"She didn't oughta have slung me out," he said suddenly. "Goddam that Fortune, if she had been a man I'd have taught her a lesson."

"She sure took advantage of her feminine sex," drawled a slim, dangerous-looking man called Eli Hawkins. "Ah reckon you shouldn't take it lyin' down, Charley. Didn't you usta tell us about that strongbox in the Wheel..."

"Funny, you seem to be thinkin' along the same trail as me," Donohue replied slowly. "I reckon I'm entitled to something after all the work I put in on the Wheel..."

The others nodded in solemn, slightly drunken, agreement.

Their heads came together while Donohue talked softly until Muller arrived with sizzling steaks. His mongrel dog, nostrils aquiver at the delicious smell, plodded at his heels.

"Here ve are chentlemen."

The men began to eat thoughtfully, only Coleman looking a little apprehensive. Donohue took a piece of meat and gave it to the dog begging at his side. It looked up into his face with affectionate eyes.

"The only trouble is that Fortune has a lot of friends..." began Coleman doubtfully. "They might make up a posse..."

Charley Donohue's eyes flicked to the small man and his lips curled in contempt.

"There ain't nothin' worthwhile that don't carry some risk," he said. "You're one of those guys who want to live for ever."

"It's all very well for you to talk, you're born goddam lucky," retorted Coleman. "'Tain't every guy who can be like you... you're a freak with a gun so you don't have to worry like other guys, ain't that so, boys?" He turned to the others who looked at him coldly.

"What you're really sayin' is you ain't got the guts to raid the Wheel," Charley Donohue said.

"You gotta be sensible about it," Coleman floundered. "Suppose we took the strong box an' they came after us... it would be a neck-tie party for us all the way the citizens here feel about Fortune. She's queen of the town."

"Who would come?" Donohue demanded. "The marshal . . . waal, he's all right when it comes to locking up drunken miners, but this would be real man's stuff, Coleman."

Donohue tossed the remainder of his steak to the dog.

"Well, they say Hannibal Reno is in these parts. Supposin' he came after us."

"Reno," Donohue cried scornfully. "That blood-money son-of-a-bitch. He wouldn't give a cuss about us unless there was a large bounty on our heads! Why, that hombre is only interested in catching poor stumblebums who have managed to get a big reward slapped on theirselves. Anyways, Coleman ..."

His words died. From round the corner of a distant shack appeared a limping figure.

"It's the hick," Eli Hawkins said in surprise. "An', by Gawd, he's totin' a shooter on his hip ..."

Donohue said nothing, but his eyes narrowed and his hands dropped down on to his thighs. The dog continued to beg beside him, but the gunman had no interest in anything but the approaching figure. Had he

50

had time to glance round, he would have seen that a number of Gila City citizens had materialised in the last few seconds and were lining the paling fence Muller had built to separate his beer garden from the street. A hush had fallen on everyone. The only sounds were the shooting of a bolt as Muller locked himself in his grog shop, and the noise of chairs falling on the sand as Donohue's companions backed away from the line of fire.

As Nathan came on his left hand strayed up to brush away the thick curtain of dark blond hair which hung over his forehead. The weight of the Peacemaker seemed strange on his leg, and added to his limp. The walk towards the beer garden seemed endless. The figure seated at the deserted table, littered with dirty dishes and half-empty beer schooners, was almost doll-like, yet the thought that within seconds he would be in range brought a fine sweat to Nathan's features.

Slowly Donohue climbed to his feet. There was a strange half smile on his face, a curious glint in his eye.

"So you had the guts to find yourself a gun, boy," he called. His hand swung close to his holster. The blood surged in his ears, every nerve was taut, the strange exhilaration of the gun-fighter filled him.

Now Nathan had reached the small gate in the far end of the garden. He kicked it open and limped through. He was walking slower now, but still steadily on. A nerve suddenly began to twitch under his left eye. He tried to remember some scrap of advice Fortune had given him.

Suddenly Donohue leapt back and kicked the edge of the table. It swung over before him and the crockery and glasses clattered to the ground, smashing each other with a noise that made the tense spectators jump.

Somewhere beyond the palings there came the

crunch of wheels. No one turned as Fortune pulled up in her smart, well-varnished buggy and watched the drama with a face which seemed drained of expression. At one stage her mouth opened as if to shout a warning, but no sound came.

Nathan stopped and stood looking bleakly at Donohue.

"Draw," he commanded.

Donohue's hand suddenly snaked to the butt of his Smith and Wesson. In a blur of speed the weapon appeared in his right hand while his left swung down so that its heel struck the hammer of the pistol. A "fanned" fusilade roared above the wrecked table.

As soon as the gunman had dropped his hand, Nathan followed suit, but his gun was still only half way out of his holster when the first bullet whistled past his cheek.

The second bullet cut a groove out of his left shoulder, but now his gun was swinging up, swinging up until there was a perfect line of sight between Nathan's eye, the sights and the crouched body of the gunman. As he pulled the trigger he was conscious of the Colt bucking with the recoil. Without thinking he dropped to one knee and sighted again, cursing the trembling of his arm.

Looking at the smoke-wreathed figure before him he saw a flash of flame from the muzzle of the Smith and Wesson, but it was a bad shot because it threw up the sand several feet to his left. It was only then that he realised the man opposite was twisting round with a strange and very graceful movement. Nathan's bullet had found its mark, Donohue was shot through the body. As he continued his slow fall Nathan fired again by some reflex action. The bullet caught the gunman and suddenly jerked him round. Donohue gave a hoarse grunt of pain and toppled sideways to the sand.

For a moment there was silence. Nathan slowly straightened up and gazed at the sprawled shape which a few seconds ago I had been his enemy. Then he began to limp forward slowly. No one else moved.

Charley Donohue was not quite dead. His fingers drew futile furrows in the sand, and when his glazing eyes saw Nathan's boots close to him he managed to turn his head and look up at the boy who had just shot him.

For a moment the two looked at each other. Donohue's white face held a slight expression of curiosity, then it went blank and his head dropped back to the sand.

The dog, who had retreated at the sound of the gunfire, returned cautiously and sniffed at the dead man. Then it began to lick the blood which was soaking through Donohue's fancy waistcoat.

Nathan continued to stand gazing down at his victim, the breeze ruffling the thick hair which had fallen back across his forehead.

His gun dropped from his hand almost as though he had forgotten its existence. His hand rose to his face which had a dazed expression of almost disbelief. Suddenly a sound came from his throat – afterwards spectators declared that he had laughed – and he turned away. Soon he began to retrace his steps through the garden.

A babble of talk followed. Men crowded round the body and someone kicked the dog hard in the ribs so it went racing away with a yelp of agony.

Nathan heard the sound of someone running over the sandy ground and turned, to see Coleman behind him with a gun in his hand. It was the bloodied Smith and Wesson which he had snatched up from beside the body of his late friend.

"Stop, you murderin' son-of-a-bitch," he cried in a shaking voice.

Nathan stopped. A hush fell on the crowd except for one voice which said: "I'll be goddamed. Look at Coleman. He sure has great personal courage when it comes to duellin' on an unarmed man."

"You killed my pard," Coleman cried, his voice almost hysterical. "Charley Donohue was the best pard I ever had ..."

As though still in a daze Nathan looked down at his hands, aware for the first time that he had dropped his new Peacemaker.

There was a brief ripple of laughter at this.

Keeping Nathan covered, Coleman, his face flushed with the pride of his new-found power, turned to the men behind him.

"I reckon we ought to string him up for what he done to Charley," he shouted.

"It was a fair fight," chimed in someone. "Charley asked for it for what he done to that kid in the Wheel."

"Don't you see – this guy was imported by Fortune to get rid of Charley," Coleman continued, inspired. "He pretended to be a hick, didn't even wear a gun in the Wheel, but he must be a professional slinger to be able to shoot Charley down like that."

There was a murmur of agreement. The remainder of Donohue's friends advanced with guns drawn.

"You're durn right, Coleman," one cried. "This was a fixed killin'. Let's string him up."

Hands gripped the dazed Nathan. Before he could resist he was dragged backwards towards the largest tree in the beer garden.

Behind him he was vaguely aware of voices raised in argument. More of Charley Donohue's friends seemed to have come forward and formed a cordon round him. Several of Gila's citizens who disagreed with Coleman surged forward angrily, but hesitated when they saw the drawn guns of the lynch gang.

"Get the sheriff," someone cried ineffectually.

Looking over the confused scene Nathan saw the black-gowned figure of Fortune stand up on her buggy. She tried to address the crowd but her voice was lost in the hubbub. Seconds later this died as a man sent a rope snaking over a branch of the tree above the boy's head.

As the noose swung by his cheek someone swiftly tied his hands behind his back, A kerchief bound his eyes.

He felt the hemp loop fitted over his head yet he hardly struggled. He was still dazed by the shooting of Donohue. It was pulled so tight he began to choke.

"Grab the end boys," Eli Hawkins cried. "Ready... a quick hoist an' we'll have seen old Charley right."

Nathan struggled and became aware that he was no longer held. He was alone in the darkness under a tree that was about to become his gibbet. The rope tightened and he was forced to stand on his toes.

A silence had frozen about him. Onlookers were speechless at the prospect of seeing him executed so soon after the killing of Donohue. Behind the tree several men gripped the rope, ready to hoist him to a painful death by strangulation.

"Stop, stop," came the voice of Fortune. "I never saw him before. I never wanted Charley killed, you must know that. You'll be killing an innocent man ... for God's sake ..."

Her voice became agonised.

"Heave," snapped Coleman. The rope tightened. Lights exploded in Nathan's brain as the hemp bit into his neck. His feet swung clear of the ground.

There was a roaring in his ears, which was sliced through by a sudden report followed by a screech of pain. From a long way away a calm voice ordered: "Let that rope go."

The rope went slack and Nathan dropped down to his knees. His chest heaved, fighting to get air down into his lungs past the restricting noose. Fingers began loosening the halter, the kerchief was whipped away from his eyes and he looked up to see Fortune. Beyond her he could see a tall man in black standing near the huddled form of Charley Donohue. A ribbon of smoke drifted lazily from the muzzle of his bone-handled revolver.

"Reno," Nathan gulped in heartfelt relief. He clambered clumsily to his feet while Fortune worked on the knots which held his wrists together. Turning he saw the men who were going to lynch him were now standing with their hands raised shoulder high. Coleman, his sleeve soaking with blood, was sobbing with the pain of his shattered arm and the loss of his importance.

"All right, fellas, there's a bullet for the first hombre to reach for his iron." Reno walked forward slowly. "There ain't gonna be no lynchin'. This guy shot Donohue fair an' square. Like the lady says, he wasn't a hired gun. He's fresh from Red Buttes sure enough, I knew him there when he was hoein' the maize patch."

There was a murmur of amusement.

"If he'd been a real slinger he'd have kept his gun in his hand," added Reno. He turned to Nathan. "Better come with me, boy," he said. Nathan nodded. As he passed the body of Charley Donohue he paused to pick up his Peacemaker. He turned to the group clustered round the hanging tree, their hands still raised.

"Any son-of-a-bitch who would like to settle the score for Donohue is more than welcome to try," he said coldly.

There was silence apart from the whimpering of the wounded Coleman. The crowd stood in awed silence as Nathan and the bounty-hunter with the tinted spectacles limped side by side from Muller's Beer Garden.

* * *

Hannibal Reno slumped down on to the bed in his dingy room with a grimace of pain. "That bullet hole Lorenz gave me ain't healed up yet, though it would have been a lot worse if it hadn't been for your Ma," he explained.

Nathan said nothing, but stood by the window, gazing out on the street below. Few people were on view, most of the citizens of Gila City having repaired to various saloons to discuss the drama of the afternoon. Absently the boy fingered his Peacemaker, clicking the cylinder round. Then he turned to the large man on the bed.

"Now, don't you bother none sayin' your piece," said Reno, lighting up a long cigar. "I jest repaid the compliment. You did the same for me at Red Buttes. Now we're quits. I like it that way. But you sure were a durned fool to drop your gun like that."

Nathan reddened.

"I ain't never shot a fella before," he replied. "I guess I felt kinda strange. I felt good – but strange." A smile showed across his usually sullen features. "When I saw Donohue fall it was like ... like ..." Words failed him.

"You ever gone with a woman?" Reno asked curiously.

Nathan shook his head.

57

"I ain't hardly seen one till I came to Gila," he confessed. "You know what it's like at Red Buttes." He shrugged.

"Yeah," said Reno. "I must tell you that sure was a pretty fine piece of gun work this afternoon. Donohue had the draw on you, but you sure shot true for a pistol shot."

"I told you," said Nathan. "I once shot an eagle out of the sky. No boasting, Mister Reno, but I got a good eye, though I was sure slow getting that gun out. When Donohue started shootin' it seemed like it would never come. I sure enough expected to die ... an' then I saw him start to fall an' I knew I'd won." Again the grin creased his face.

"Careful you don't get to enjoy it too much," said Reno. "You were lucky with Charley Donohue. He shot like he wore his clothes... he was flashy. Fanning looks smart but unless you're close up it ain't worth much. If you'd been against a guy as fast as Donohue but with a cool eye it'd be you they be ridin' out to Boothill. You're a rifleman, not a slinger."

"I can learn," Nathan muttered. "Mister Reno, why did you quit Red Buttes without sayin' goodbye ..."

"Your Ma was good to me," said Reno. "She asked me to go. She knew you were plumb fired on coming along with me. Like all mothers, she didn't want to lose you. Still, you quit anyways ..."

"Yeah. I wanted to catch you up. I was lookin' for you when Donohue had some fun at my expense in the Wheel of Fortune. I jest had to come back and even things up."

"I was holed up here," said Reno. "That wound still is awkward. I didn't go on the streets 'cause I didn't want folks to know I was in town. There's often someone who would like to pay back an old score, or mebbe prove he's better with an iron than me. What are you gonna do now, boy?"

"You know what I want, Mister Reno," said Nathan. "An" please don't keep callin' me 'boy.' I don't feel like I was a boy no more."

"Waal," Reno drawled thoughtfully, "I got a word of advice to you – move on, go back to Red Buttes mebbe, but get away from this territory. You're now the fella who shot down Good-time Charley Donohue who was the top gun in this town. How long do you reckon it'll be before some guy wants to become the fella who gunned down Nathan Knight. Get out while you can. This gun fightin' is a crazy game . . ."

"You do all right."

"It ain't a game with me, it's a way I make my livin'," the big man replied. "I don't give a cuss about reputation unless it unnerves the guy I'm goin' after. Anyways, boy, you should forget any ideas of bein' a gunman. You ain't cut out for it...if you was a natural you'd never have dropped your gun. Havin' a straight eye is only part of it. You gotta be born with a gun-fighter's heart. Go back to Red Buttes... you owe it to your Ma."

Nathan grimaced. "You're just a-sayin' that cause she fixed that bullet hole in you, Mister Reno."

Reno removed his tinted glasses and polished them with a black silk kerchief.

"Mebbe," he said at last. "But I figure you quit Red Buttes because I came along. I don't want to be the guy who started you on the sundown trail . . ."

"The sundown trail . . ."

"A figure of speech. The sundown trail leads only into night."

"Just a minute," said Nathan. "In that newspaper piece on you. In it they called you 'Reno of the Sundown Trail'... what did they mean by that?"

"Nothin'," said Reno. "It was jest what some loco newspaper writer wrote. Hell, those guys write anythin' if they think it makes their article more interestin'."

"But what made him think of it... seems kinda strange to me," Nathan seemed suddenly very interested.

Reno reflected a moment.

"By a coincidence, it has usually been at sundown when I've taken a man," he said slowly. "I guess that newspaper guy – funny little fella he was by the name of Milton Homer – thought it was some sort of tag he could put on me."

"The Sundown Trail," mused Nathan, "Sounds good, Mister Reno. I guess I still want to ride it with you."

"I told you boy, I'm a loner. I've always worked that way. I don't want no-one, and least of all a guy that drops his gun. Look at yourself, boy, you're a farmer by Gawd. That's your life. Go back to it, in the fullness of time marry a good woman, raise your kids and live out your life the way the Lord intended."

"You're gettin' to sound like a, preacher, Mister Reno. But you don't practise what you preach."

"The Lord has different ways for us to follow," said Reno. "Once I thought my destiny was to be a farmer, but the Lord planned different."

"Why, is there more money in collectin' bounties?"

Reno's lips drew back in a tight line.

"Listen, Knight," he hissed. "If you was anyone else I'd throw you out that window, but you're so plumb ignorant I just pity you. Now get out. We've done our business together. We're square, leave it that way."

White-faced, Nathan shook his head.

"I ain't leavin' you, Mister Reno," he said softly. "This afternoon I proved I ain't just no farm hand. I killed Charley Donohue in fair fight. You've gotta realise I can be useful to you. In fact, Mister Reno, you'll take me because you have to ..."

Reno laughed without mirth.

"I'd rather take along a sick houn' dawg," he said. "Why the hell should I take you along when I don't need no one."

Nathan walked across the creaking floor and stood over the reclining man.

"You're lyin' when you say you don't need anyone," he snapped. "You need me, Mister Reno. You need me because you're goin' t

CHAPTER FIVE

At Nathan's words, Reno looked up with a bleak expression on his features. The boy noticed that his right hand had slid close to his gunbelt. "That's a mighty funny remark you just made," he said. "I guess you got your loop round some fancy idea simply 'cause I wear these glasses. But do you really reckon I could carry on my trade if there was somethin' wrong with my sight? What gave you such a crazy notion?"

Nathan regarded him coldly.

"It's no good trying to bluff your way out of it, Mister Reno," he said, trying to control his voice so he sounded calm. "I guess it took me a while to put everythin' together but right from the start I guessed there was somethin' strange about you. Even when I first saw you, when you shot down Lorenz I thought it was a mite funny that a gunfighter like you – who could make a perfect border shift – needed to use so many bullets. If you could make a shift like that, there'd have been no need to use it against one fella.

"Them glasses you wear ain't just ordinary glasses to stop the glare of the sun – they've got lenses same as those bad-sighted people wear. And then there's a bit in that newspaper story about you, Reno ... and the Sundown Trail. Now I've figured why you always take your man at sundown. That sort of light gives you the best advantage, specially if you can get your man between

62

you and the sun."

Reno's hand closed on the bone handle of his Peacemaker.

"You seem to have been figurin' a lot, boy," he drawled. "Maybe you know too much. If I'd any sense I'd shoot you down like a dawg where you stand 'cause it's a mighty dangerous thing you're sayin' even if there's no truth in it."

"There's truth in it all right, Reno," Nathan declared. "An' that's why you need me. I can shoot damn straight and my eyes are good. With me beside you you wouldn't need to fear more. You wouldn't need to be scairt of bein' ambushed by someone you couldn't see properly. You need to get close enough to your man. So you have to take him with your Colt. I could pick out a fella for you at a thousand yards."

Reno smiled slightly but without humour. "You got it all figured out, ain't you, boy?" "I sure have, Reno," Nathan said. "Right from the time I saw you ride up the trail from Red Buttes, I knew I wanted to go along with you. Now I reckon I could be as much use to you as you could be to me. An'... an' you won't scare me off by holdin' on to your pistol."

"Supposin' the answer is still no," said Reno. "What would you do then, boy?"

"I'd tell the world," said Nathan. "Think what that would mean, Reno. The great Hannibal Reno goin' blind! Why, there must be dozens of guys with scores to settle with you who, once they knew that, would be hot on your trail."

"That's an ugly way to go about it. An' it's an ugly way for a guy to talk when I just saved your life."

"Maybe," said Nathan, "but I guess you understand I'm a desperate man. I've seen what I want to be and nothin's gonna stop me."

Suddenly, surprisingly, Reno laughed. His hand loosened on the butt of his Colt and he slapped his thigh in a gesture of good humour.

"Goddammit boy, I must say I like your courage. But the joke's over now. There ain't nothin' wrong with my eyes. If there had been I wouldn't have been able to shoot that guy who was aimin' to hang you this afternoon. So you must admit my sight is dandy."

"I heard tell," Nathan said in his expressionless voice, "that there's some kinds of eye trouble that only come on from time to time. One day you can see good, the next you're damn near blind. I guess that's the kind you've got. There's a story that Hickock has the same trouble."

Suddenly he leaned forward, snatched Reno's spectacles from his face and danced back into a dark corner of the room. With an oath Reno drew his Colt and held it uncertainly.

"There you are," hissed Nathan triumphantly. "If I'd been standing between you and the window you'd have had a bullet through me by now. But I'm in the shadow and you ain't got a' bead on me properly, Reno."

Wearily, Reno rubbed his hand across his inflamed eyes.

"Okay, boy, give 'em back. If I'd really wanted to shoot you I could have got you from the sound of your voice. I guess you're right about my eyes. It's been gettin' worse and worse over the last

64

few months. Like you said, comin' on in spasms. The doc I saw has some fancy name for it. Sometimes I think I'll save up a big pile of money an' go East, or even across to Europe and see if some of them fancy eye doctors can't do somethin' to fix me up. For God's sake don't tell a soul outside this room. As you said, there's many a guy who'd find the guts to gun me if I couldn't see him properly."

"I won't breathe a word, Reno. As long as I can come along with you."

"Okay, boy," Reno said with a sigh. "Let's give it a try. You've proved to me you've got more guts than I ever thought. You can take a third of the reward money. But if it don't work out between us, let's split up when I say so. Is that agreed?"

"It surely is, Reno," declared Nathan, almost laughing in his delight. "I'll be so darned useful to you, you'll want to keep me on all right."

He handed the tinted spectacles back to the bounty hunter. "When do we go after our first man, Reno?"

"You sound like you're anxious for blood, boy. But I guess there won't be anything doing for a little while yet. For one thing, Doc Williams tells me I'll have to rest my leg for a while otherwise that wound will open when I get on a horse. Secondly. I'm waiting here on some information which may lead to somethin' pretty big."

Nathan nodded, still smiling because he knew he was going to be apprenticed to the game of man-hunting.

"You'd better get a room in this place," Reno added. "I'll have to set about teachin' you how to pull your gun out of your holster without taking all day about it. You've got a lot to learn, boy. So don't start gettin' any fancy notions just because you managed to down Charley Donohue."

At that moment the door of the room swung back and Fortune Sarrat walked in. Ignoring the black-clad figure of Reno stretched out on the bed, the girl looked coolly at Nathan as he stood by the window, idly clicking the chamber of the Colt which had so recently ended the career of Donohue.

"Getting ready to carve your first notch on the grip?" she asked.

Nathan shook his head. "No, miss," he replied quietly.

"You were very lucky this afternoon," the girl gambler told him. "You've missed death twice since I saw you this morning. Another few inches and Charley's bullet would have got you." She nodded at the bloodstained crease on Nathan's shirt. "How do you feel, now that you've killed a man?"

"Good. I feel goddamed *good*. I'm happy I'm still alive an' he's dead. What d'you want me to say? That I'm sorry for him? I know he was your friend once, but. . ."

Fortune's eyes flicked away for a moment.

"Yes," she murmured. "I guess I'd forgotten that until I saw him a-layin' there. He was a fool though. He thought he could take over the Wheel of Fortune because I found him... amusing. Don't you see, I had to put him in his place."

"I guess you did, Miss Fortune," Nathan said drily. "I guess you must be pretty pleased the way it's ended up."

She shook her head but said nothing.

"I guess I can understand now why you took an interest out at Boothill this mornin'," he continued.

"If you think that, you're a fool," Fortune snapped. "But I didn't come here to discuss Donohue with you. I've got a proposition to make to you. Strangely enough, you're regarded as the top gunman in this town because you shot down Good-time Charley. I need somebody at the Wheel with a reputation as a gunslinger just to keep the clients in order. I'm offering you the job, Knight."

"You want I should take over Charley Donohue's job?"

She nodded. "That's about the size of it. The pay's good."

"Thank you for askin', miss," said Nathan, "but me and Reno here..." he glanced towards the bounty hunter, but Reno shook his head slightly. Fortune shifted her gaze towards him.

"What have you got to do with it?" she demanded. "I reckon you'll be moving on soon enough – as soon as you can find some poor wretch with a reward on his head. I must tell you that I don't think much of men like you who see human life in terms of money."

"I don't want to argue with a pretty lady like you," Reno drawled, "but I don't figure the owner of a gamblin' saloon is in a position to get high an' mighty on the question of ethics."

"You've got it wrong," said Fortune. "There's a big difference between you an' me, man. It's a tough life out here for a lot of folks. I give them something they're missing. A little comfort, a little excitement, a chance for a good time. Maybe a chance to win themselves a pile at cards. Without this, their lives would be hellish monotonous. But you, *you* deal in death." She turned back to Nathan.

"I don't want to stay in this company," she said abruptly. "Will you come and work for me at the Wheel?"

"Happy to, miss," Nathan grinned. "When do you want me to start?"

"Tomorrow night. It might not be tactful tonight. I guess a few of Charley's old friends will be getting pretty liquored up. It'll be different after he's been buried."

"Okay." Nathan said. "An' I'd be obliged if you'd keep back my wages until that handout you gave me is repaid."

"You're a proud young crittur, aren't you? I'll hold back the money if it makes you feel better," Fortune said. "But there's one thing I'd like you to do before you come to the Wheel."

"What's that?" asked Nathan.

"Get your goddamned hair cut." She walked out of the room.

* * *

Next day was a high point in Nathan's life. Still limping slightly from his smashed toe, he strolled the streets of Gila City, comforted by the unfamiliar weight of the gun on his thigh, and feeling a secret enjoyment when loafers looked at him with a certain respect. Here and there he was pointed out as though he was somebody of importance. The lonely, sullen years of his life at Red Buttes were slipping away.

At last he found the store he was looking

for – the Hard Cash Elegant Clothing Emporium. As he walked inside he was conscious of the noise his heavy farm boots made on the wooden floor. A young, exquisitely dressed clerk behind the counter looked at him with obvious distaste.

"Good morning, *sir"* he began sarcastically. "What would it be my pleasure to serve you?"

"I want an outfit," announced Nathan. "I wanna hat, coat, shirt, pants – the lot!"

"I must warn you," said the clerk, "that the garments for sale in this emporium are from the East, and they are expensive. If it's denims you want, I suggest you try the General Store down the road."

"I don't want no store denims," Nathan replied patiently. "But if you ain't too keen on serving me, I ..."

At that moment the proprietor of the emporium appeared at the door and, seeing Nathan standing there, urgently beckoned the clerk over to him. For a moment there was a whispered conversation and then the clerk returned, the supercilious smile wiped from his pasty face.

"Excuse me, sir," he apologised to Nathan. "I'm sure we can fit you out – er – very nicely." He looked down at the gun strapped to Nathan's thigh and a slight shudder went through his frame. ".... I'm very sorry, sir, I didn't recognise you when you first walked in. Now, sir, if you'll come over here I'll show you our latest line in shirts and we'll build up from there."

Half an hour later Nathan walked out into the hot glare of the Gila City street. Gone were his patched denims, his clumsy boots and faded, work-stained shirt. In its place he wore an outfit of black in faithful imitation of Reno. His shirt was of the finest silk, as indeed was the kerchief knotted round his neck. His feet were encased in shiny high-heeled boots, while on his head he wore a black broad-brimmed hat that threw the upper part of his face into dark shadow. Over his shirt he wore a frock coat of fashionable city cut, the right side buttoned back to give quick access to his gun.

Grinning inwardly at the thought of being well dressed for the first time in his life, he limped along the boardwalk in the direction of a barber's shop.

"Guess Miss Fortune will hardly recognise me when I start work tonight," he thought with shy pleasure.

The Italian barber manfully snipped away at his thatch of fair hair. When he was finished, he held up a mirror for Nathan to inspect the effect. Instead of a sullen-faced country boy with hair hanging over his eyes, Nathan saw the face of a determined young man, with a broad forehead, cool pale blue eyes and hair slicked back with grease. It would have been doubtful if anyone would have recognised him as the yokel who, a few days ago, had been hoeing by the maize patch when Hannibal Reno had ridden into his life along the Red Buttes trail.

CHAPTER SIX

The soft light that illuminated the green surfaced card tables reflected on Fortune Sarrat's regular features which were framed by long tresses of dark hair. With a thin cheroot between her lips, she deftly dealt a poker hand to a circle of clients who had come to try their luck at the Wheel of Fortune. They were a motley collection of men, a burly well-dressed cattle buyer with a seamed face and a roll of money which made a bulge in his pocket; a miner with calloused hands and stained tartan shirt; a young cowboy with a youthful determination to double his month's roll, and a traveller in patent medicines whose soft white fingers Fortune was beginning to distrust.

One thing they did have in common was the avid gaze with which they regarded the cards Fortune expertly flicked towards them. When each man had his hand Fortune raised her eyes, looking at the far end of her saloon. There, unobtrusively in a corner (where he had received his humiliation on the first night of his arrival) stood Nathan Knight. It was hard for Fortune to imagine him as he had been when she first brought him over for a drink, having taken pity on his uncertainty and farmhand clothes. Now he lounged against the bar, a slim, stylish figure in his black clothes, his eyes casually roving round the large room with an assurance which Fortune knew had only come by the slaying of Goodtime Charley Donohue.

The man at the honky-tonk piano struck up a tune and there was the pleasing sound of laughter throughout the Wheel of Fortune.

The bidding at Fortune's table began. Little towers of silver appeared on the baize which, at the end of the round, the traveller drew towards himself with a smile of innocent satisfaction.

"I sure do seem to be lucky tonight, gents," he remarked. "It ain't often I play this game, but I sure am enjoyin' it."

"That's fine," smiled Fortune. "We like to see the customers happy here. Tell me, sir, what is your – um – line of business?"

"Madam, I travel in Doctor Hinklebaum's snake oil and rheumatism cure," he announced. "I can tell you, madam, that it's a pretty fine medicine for anything from the colic to heart failure. It's mighty good for rheumatism too, and there's many miners in this state who will testify to that. Made entirely from a secret recipe known only to the Doctor Hinklebaum – of whom no doubt everybody has heard if they have an interest in scientific matters. As well as being good for human beings it's mighty good for cattle, only you have to give them a mite larger dose. We do a special large bottle for farmers. Doctor Hinklebaum's preparation is dandy for the staggers or bloat."

"My, that's interesting," said Fortune charmingly, "Perhaps I should have a bottle myself just in case I get the staggers some time."

There was a laugh round the table but the purveyor of medicine ignored it.

"It'll be my pleasure, madam, to present you with our extra large size family bottle."

"I think it's your deal," said Fortune and watched while the traveller's white fingers began to shuffle the cards. He did it a little clumsily, apologising to the others by saying that he wasn't much used to card-playing and they would have to bear with him. After a while the barman came over and replenished the players' drinks. Just as he was about to go Fortune gave him an almost imperceptible nod. Back at the bar the man leaned forward and whispered a couple of words to Nathan.

Unhurriedly Nathan drained his glass of sarsaparilla then began an aimless walk across the hall, looking over a card player's shoulder here or exchanging a word with a tinsel-costumed hostess there. Soon he was close to Fortune's table, and for a while stood watching the game with the vague interest that people have in cards when they are not actually betting money.

After a couple of hands the young cowboy threw down his cards and declared that he was cleaned out. He tried desperately to sound light-hearted about it although inwardly he was furious that he should have lost a month's pay in the space of a couple of hours.

"That's bad luck," Fortune said, smiling at him. "But do have a couple of drinks on me before you leave." She made a signal to the bar. "Next time you come in you may make a pile that will keep people talking for weeks. That's the way it is with cards."

The young man got up and walked towards the bar, his admiration for Fortune struggling with his feeling of acute disappointment at the idea of having to work hard for another month before he could feel a roll of money in his hip pocket. Nathan casually sat down in the vacant chair.

"Hope you don't mind if I join," he remarked

73

pleasantly. The other players nodded without speaking.

Soon it was the turn of the traveller to deal again. Nathan watched as he clumsily shuffled the cards. He dropped one, apologised to the company and shuffled again.

"I do beg pardon, folks," he said. "It's only since I've come West that I've actually started to play. I haven't had much practice yet."

"You look as if you've been doing all right, friend," said Nathan, nodding at the money before him.

"Beginner's luck, sir, beginner's luck," laughed the traveller, and he began to deal, putting the cards carefully face down in front of each player, not with the practised flick that Fortune, or others used to card gambling, employed. Nathan picked up his cards, spread them out fanwise and laid them down again with a look of disgust on his features. When the bidding began he said he would pass.

"There ain't a durned thing I can do with that hand," he grumbled. If he had a bad hand, others seemed to think that their luck was in. The bidding continued, piles of silver dollars were pushed forward into the centre of the table. Up and up the bets rose until finally the cattle-buyer looked up at the traveller and said: "I'll see you."

With an almost childlike expression of delight the traveller laid out a full house for all to see. The cattle buyer grunted in disgust and did not even bother to show his cards. He leaned back in his chair and lit a cigar with resignation.

"Well, well, I must say this is almost as profitable as selling Dr. Hinklebaum's snake oil and rheumatism cure," chuckled the traveller, scooping his winnings into a heap. "It has been a lucky night for me, gentlemen, and I thank you very much. But I have a hard day ahead of me tomorrow and I think I must really turn in now."

Before he could finish his sentence Nathan's hand clamped down on his wrist.

"Before you go," he hissed, "there's something I'd like to ask you about the way you play cards."

"What d'you mean?" cried the traveller, half rising and struggling to free his wrist from the vice-like grip.

"Its about this luck of yours," said Nathan. "Now to my mind it seems that you were just a little bit too lucky."

Talk at nearby tables died away and eyes swivelled towards Nathan and the traveller.

"Are you suggesting there was something wrong in the way I played cards?" demanded the traveller.

"I'm suggesting you were mighty lucky," retorted Nathan. "Almost too lucky if you were to ask me."

With a sudden movement, the traveller wrenched his hand free and jerked back.

"Are you calling me a cheat?" he cried. "I am."

"You're a liar," said the traveller and, as though by magic, a small double-barrelled Derringer pistol appeared in his right hand. Silence fell on the Wheel of Fortune. The traveller had just uttered the West's greatest insult and everyone knew it was usually followed by fast action. Nathan slowly rose to his feet, his eyes on the traveller's face rather than on the small pistol which was aimed unerringly at his stomach.

"You're a mighty clever fellow with your sleeves," Nathan remarked.

"Because I carry a gun in my sleeve it doesn't mean I'm a card cheat," the traveller retorted. "A man's got to protect himself against bullies like you. And though my gun is pretty small I guess you know at this distance even a Derringer slug is a pretty painful proposition."

Nathan nodded. The tone of the traveller's voice, which had changed dramatically from his earlier light-hearted tone, told him that here was a man who would not hesitate to shoot.

"Now if you care to apologise," said the traveller, "'I guess I'll collect my winnings, go on my way and we won't have any more trouble here."

"Folk always seem to be askin' me to apologise in this place," Nathan muttered, "but – uh – I guess you're right, mister. Here, take your winnin's."

With his right hand he scooped up a handful of dollars from the table where the traveller had been sitting. Holding them out in front of him, he took a step forward. The traveller eyed him with a look of puzzlement on his face. Suddenly Nathan's hand swept upwards and a shower of silver shot into the traveller's face. As it did so the traveller'sd finger jerked on the trigger of the toy pistol. He had lost his aim and the bullet shattered an engraved mirror.

Meanwhile Nathan had drawn his Colt. It swept in an arc and the long blue steel barrel hit the side of the traveller's neck with a sickening thud. With a moan the man slumped to the floor while Nathan holstered his gun. Then he knelt down beside the unconscious man. From his left sleeve he drew a card which he held up for all to see. From, the patrons of the Wheel of Fortune saloon there came a roar, partly of anger and partly of laughter. Without saying another word Nathan walked back to his place at the bar while the body of the limp card-sharp was unceremoniously dragged away.

"Well, gentlemen," said Fortune coolly, "shall we continue our game? I reckon we ought to put our friend's winnings in the pot."

The men agreed. Fortune waved over the young cowboy who had lost his money.

"I think you ought to take a hand in this." she said, "seeing you were losing money against a cheat all evening."

He smiled his agreement and sat down again. A minute later the Wheel of Fortune echoed to his triumphant yell as he scooped in money which the late purveyor of Dr. Hinklebaum's medicine had earlier won. Not quite knowing what to do, the boy blurted out, "Drinks for everyone on me."

There was a wild stampede to the bar.

Later that night, the young cowboy was broke again. But this time he had a monumental hangover to go with it. While the barmen were busy catering for the thirsts of their patrons at the unexpected bonanza, one of the dancing girls came and whispered in Nathan's ear that Fortune wanted to see him in her office.

"Come in," she said, when he tapped on the door panel. He entered and saw her sitting behind a large desk. Her face, in the soft light of the shaded kerosene lamp, looked startlingly beautiful and his heart seemed to beat a little more rapidly.

"You handled that very well, Nathan," Fortune said. "I'm getting my money's worth out of you."

He nodded seriously.

"Tonight is pay night," she added, pushing notes and silver across the desk towards him. "It's all right," she added. "I've already deducted that handout which you seem to resent so much," she smiled up at him. "Do you like working for me, Nathan?"

He nodded. "It's better than hoeing the bean patch," he said.

She laughed. "It's funny," she said. "Only two weeks have passed but I can hardly remember what you looked like when you came in here that first night."

"I'm pleased about that," said Nathan. Not knowing what to say, his eyes roved around the office and lighted on a large steel box. "If that's where you keep your money, miss, you ought to have it bolted to the floor," he said.

"That's where I keep my money," she replied. "I don't trust banks. I've seen too many go bust." She signed. "It was a bank going bust that wiped out my old home," she said. "I come from New Mexico originally. My father had a nice place until it was lost through a bank. When we had to leave it broke his heart – he was never the same man after. He'd lost the heart to live."

"I think I know what you mean," he said. "Something like that happened to my own folk in Red Buttes."

"So me and my brother we had to find our way as best we could," said Fortune. "I found that I had a streak for gamblin' and here I am. And now you know why I don't trust banks," she added. She lit herself a slim cheroot and blew out a cloud of smoke.

"You don't like me smoking these things, do you?" she asked.

"It's none of my business what you do," Nathan replied. "It did seem kinda strange at first to see a – er – well – er – a pretty lady like you smoking like a man."

"Yes," she said, "but then you don't often see a... pretty lady dealing at monte or faro. And do you really think I'm pretty, Nathan?" She leaned back in her chair, watching his face with a quizzical expression in her eyes, slightly amused at his awkwardness.

"Sure, miss, I think you're pretty. In fact, I – er, I think you're er – " Words failed him. He stood in front of her, his money in his hand'.

"Would you like to have supper with me tonight, Nathan?" asked Fortune.

"I don't know," he replied, fidgeting.

"What do you mean, you don't know? Either you would like to have supper with me or you wouldn't."

"Well, I'm your hired gunman, aren't I? I don't want to be no – " He looked about him as though trying to pick the right words. "I don't want to be another Goodtime Charley Donohue."

A cold look came into Fortune's eyes. "That was a mean, lowdown, goddamn lousy thing to say," she hissed. "I was wrong about you, Nathan. You've got smart clothes on, but you're still a hick. You just don't know kindness when you see it."

79

"Maybe you're right, miss," he mumbled awkwardly. "I seem to do things wrong with you. Perhaps I'd better quit this job. I guess you knew I wouldn't really want to stay long anyway."

"You want to go with that – that friend of yours, that Reno, the blood-money man Is that it?"

"We did figure we might ride the trail a bit together," said Nathan.

Fortune rose from her desk and walked round and stood in front of Nathan. "No good ever comes of riding the trail with a man like that," she said. "What has he got to offer that you wouldn't find at the Wheel of Fortune?"

"It's hard to put into words, miss," said Nathan. "I don't know how to say it. It's just that I remember him ridin' up a trail. It was near sundown and he was just ridin' along and I suddenly knew that he was what I wanted to be. I hadn't ever seen anybody like him before."

"So. You want to be a professional killer? I guess I must have been pretty mistaken about you."

"Sounds bad the way you say it," Nathan admitted. "You call him a professional killer. But sheriffs and marshals are professional killers, an' so are soldiers."

"It's their duty," said Fortune. "His duty is only to make money."

"I can't hardly see a professional soldier refusin' his pay," Nathan said. He pushed the money into his trouser pocket. "I guess I'd better say goodnight, miss," he added. "I don't seem to have pleased you much after all."

She threw her cigar down on to the floor. Suddenly her arms were round his neck, pulling his

80

face down to hers. With eyes closed, she kissed him on the mouth. It was the first time Nathan had ever been kissed by a girl in his life. His heart pounded with the same exciting, almost sick, feeling which he had experienced as he walked towards Charley Donohue. For a moment he stood with his arms hanging at his sides, feeling the warmth of Fortune's lips against his. Then his arms enfolded her. She drew back her face and laughed at him.

"There ain't no need to break my back," she said. "You've still got a lot of things to learn apart from how to draw a gun."

CHAPTER SEVEN

It was noon as Nathan Knight walked along the boardwalk under the verandahs of the buildings which made up the main street of Gila City. The heat was intense and dust devils, blown on the hot desert wind, spun down the rutted thoroughfare. Loafers, who were sitting in small untalking groups in the deepest shade of the verandahs, looked up with interest as the young man walked past. For a moment he was the subject of their conversation, a slight relief in the endless boredom of those who spent their lives watching the world go by from the shadows. By now Nathan was used to being pointed at. Not only was he famous for the fact that he had shot down Charley Donohue, but also for the way he carried out his work as gunslinger for Fortune Sarrat at the Wheel of Fortune. Even the marshal gave him a surly nod now, intimating that he had got over his displeasure at the way Nathan had double-crossed him by leaping from the coach.

Nathan had just been with Hannibal Reno, who spent nearly all his time stretched out in his room, while his wound continued to heal. Nathan discovered that he passed his hours by reading the Bible. He seemed particularly fond of the Old Testament.

"There are some darn good yarns here," he had explained to Nathan, when Nathan looked surprised to see what he was reading, no doubt trying to equate his mother's religious fanaticism and "Bible-bangin'" with Reno's taste in Biblical literature. Nathan was relieved that Reno showed no sign of going back on the idea of their partnership. And he began to get the feeling that Reno himself was pleased at the idea of a companion now his spells of eye trouble were becoming more and more frequent. Nevertheless Nathan knew he would be relieved when he and Reno hit the trail together. To him his job at the Wheel of Fortune was merely a way of making money to get himself outfitted before he started his career as a bounty hunter. Now, on this day following the unmasking of the cardsharp, he was strangely disturbed. His thoughts kept straying back to the slim beautiful figure of Fortune and he came near to blushing as he remembered the warmth of her lips against his. Having had no experience with women he was shrewd enough to know that while he could probably make a fool of himself over Fortune, she was probably the very last girl he should get entangled with. There was something feline and dangerous about her which, in a strange way, added to her fascination. He wished he could talk to somebody about her. It had crossed his mind to mention it to Reno but when the time came he felt too embarrassed. He thought that if he told Reno how he felt, the bounty hunter might decide he was not dedicated enough to be his companion. Through his muddled thoughts came his own words of the night before which had upset Fortune so much, rather like some refrain. "I don't want to be another Goodtime Charley Donohue." Perhaps this girl gambler made a habit of amusing herself with all her gunslingers. Nathan wondered who had carried a gun for her before Goodtime Charley.

He was so immersed in his thoughts that he

almost stumbled into someone coming in the opposite direction. He stood back, and saw, standing before him, the girl called Victoria Grayson who had helped him to escape when he had been hiding in the arroyo.

"I beg your pardon, ma'am," he said, removing his hat. "But I'm mighty glad I've bumped into you just the same. I always hoped I'd meet you again so I could thank you for what you did when I jumped off that stage."

Victoria, who was wearing a pretty white muslin frock, looked at him coldly.

"If I had known how things were going to turn out, I would not have helped you one little bit," she said. "I thought I was helping you to get away from something instead of which you merely wanted to come and shoot a man down. I was certainly mistaken about you. I thought you were a nice farm boy in some sort of trouble. But now we can see exactly what you are. You're like the rest of them, full of violence and arrogance because of that instrument of death you wear strapped on your leg."

As she spoke a flush of anger had risen to her cheek, making her appear more attractive. Nathan, taken aback by her outburst, hardly knew how to reply.

"I understand that you're the hired gun at the Wheel of Fortune Saloon," she continued. "That must be a fine job, lording it over everyone while they get drunk and lose their money at cards and are taken in by that – that – "

"You sound mighty hard, ma'am," observed Nathan. "I don't think things are quite the way you picture them. Every man has a right to carry a gun for self defence. Miss Fortune's gambling saloon ain't all that bad. A lot of men have hard lives here. They have no womenfolk of their own, nothing to do at nights. This gives them a little bit of fun in their hard lives."

"It's no good trying to justify yourself to me," said Victoria. "You are already on the road that so many have travelled. William Bonney, Hickock, Saul Powers; all men who have got reputations with their guns. And what have they done to build up this fine new country? They have only caused destruction and death. The real heroes are the men who build the railroads, who look for gold and open up new towns, who drive in cattle, and who start farms."

"You certainly feel very strongly about it, ma'am," said Nathan, smiling at her. "But really I ain't as bad as you seem to think."

"Well, there is no point in carrying the conversation further," said Victoria. "I must get back to my school."

"You're the schoolmarm, are you?" said Nathan.

"Yes, I am the teacher here," Victoria replied. "When you saw me on the coach that day, I was going with my aunt to visit a sick relative. And can I tell you one thing, Knight, which I am sure will make you very proud, but which makes me terribly unhappy. At school my little boys have wooden guns and they play at being Nathan Knight. They draw lots as to who is to be you, who is to be Donohue. So already you are infecting others by your violence. Good-day to you."

She stepped past him and continued down the boardwalk. Nathan turned and watched her go and shook his head. "The way she goes on anyone would think I was Jesse James, or somethin'," he muttered. As he watched, the girl slowed, then stopped. She seemed to stand for a moment as though in thought, then turned and slowly walked back to the young man. When she reached him she looked at him frankly in the face.

"Perhaps I should apologise, Knight," she said. "I guess you are no worse than many of the others around here. It is just when I saw my pupils imitating you I felt very angry but that did not give me the right to be rude to you. If ever you are passing the schoolhouse look in, and I will know that you have forgiven me." Without another word she turned on her heel and strode briskly away.

Nathan shook his head once more. Women were something he just could not begin to understand, and he longed to get away into the clear-cut world of Hannibal Reno. Yet, the next day he did stop by at the schoolhouse.

* * *

There was a light tap at the door of Reno's room. Instinctively his large hand slid down to where his gun lay within easy reach on the floor beside his bed.

"Who is it?" he called.

On the other side of the door came a voice. "My name is Ethan Holcomb. I represent the *Gila City Sentinel*. I was wondering if I could have a few words with you, Reno."

Reno sighed. He took off his tinted glasses and rubbed the back of his hand across his bloodshot eyes which today were troubling him. Then he leaned over and pulled back the bolt to allow the door to open.

A tall, scrawny man in a rusty frock coat entered, holding an ancient derby in his hand. He

86

reached the centre of the room, and then stood awkwardly as though not quite knowing what to do next.

"Sit down, mister," Reno invited, nodding towards a chair. Gratefully Holcomb sat down, carefully placed his hat on the floor beside him, then drew forth a notebook and a pencil. The pencil was dwarfed by his huge hands.

"Uh – I am a journalist with the – ah – *Gila City Sentinel"* he explained. "I would be mighty appreciative if I could have a few words from you."

"Why?"

"Uh, well, Reno, you're a pretty famous man, and I'd like to tell our readers just what you happen to be doing in their city. Can you tell me what you're doing here?"

"Restin'."

Meticulously, the man inscribed the word "resting," then looked up. "How do you mean, resting?" he asked.

"Like this – a-layin' on a bed," said Reno. "Restin'. I had some trouble with my leg so I'm restin' it."

The man wrote down the word "leg."

"Are you on – uh, what shall we say – business here, Reno?"

"No."

"Perhaps you're planning to settle down in our fair town?"

"No."

"Is it true that – " The reporter looked wildly round the room as though for inspiration. "Is it true that you have shot – uh – twenty men, Reno?"

"No."

"Could you tell me about the – uh – relationship between you and the young man you saved from hanging after the Donohue shooting? Some folks seem to figure he's a personal friend of yours. Is it true, for example, that you taught him how to use a gun?"

Reno's head moved in a gesture which could have meant anything.

"Reno," said Holcomb, rubbing hard at the back of his scrawny neck. "You're said to be a – uh – top bounty hunter. I'd appreciate anything you could tell me about this occupation that – uh – would be of interest to our readers."

"There ain't nothin' I can say. It's a job."

"Is it true that this young man, this Nathan Knight, is likely to join you in your – uh – profession?"

"Has he said so?"

Holcomb sadly shook his head.

"No, I'm afraid he's not very forthcoming, Reno. What he did say I'm afraid I could not print in the *Sentinel.*"

Reno smiled slightly, but said nothing. Holcomb looked dispiritedly at his large boots. Then with a final effort, he said: "Who in your opinion is the best gunman in the South-west, Reno?"

"I've no idea. Mebbe Saul Powers."

"Have you ever shot it out with him?" asked the reporter with faint hope.

"No. I ain't even seen him."

"Finally," sighed the journalist, "have you got a – uh – message for the citizens of Gila City. I sure would appreciate it if you could give me *something* to print."

"Yeah, I've got a message."

The reporter bent down over him hopefully, ready to record the golden words.

"I'm ready, Reno."

"My message to the citizens of Gila City is this," said Reno. "Tell the sons-of-bitches I wish they'd keep their goddamn dogs quiet at night. The way they howl in this town is something disgraceful. A man can't hardly get to sleep. It's the most dog-howlingest town I've ever had the bad luck to be in. How's that for a message for the citizens of Gila?"

Sorrowfully the newspaper man closed his notebook. For a moment his lips trembled as if he was fighting to say something. But as his eye noted the bone handled revolver lying close to Reno's bed, he bit back his remarks and stood up.

"Uh – thank you – uh – very much, Reno," he said.

"You're welcome," said Reno graciously. "I'd like to see a proof before you print the interview."

Suddenly Holcomb's eyes shone as he remembered something. "One last thing before I go," he said. "Why is it, Reno, that a newspaper article once described you as riding the – uh – Sundown Trail?"

Reno looked at him blankly.

"I couldn't begin to guess," he said, "Unless I was headin' for a place called Sundown."

Holcomb clamped his stained hat firmly on his head and walked out, red-faced at having failed to get what he had hoped to be his lead story for that week's issue of the *Sentinel*. He had left a big space on the front page for it, and now he wondered how in tarnation he could fill it. Little did he know that he was soon to get a lead story that would have eclipsed anything the famous Reno could have told him even if he had wanted to.

Back in his room Reno carefully locked the door and settled back with his Bible. Soon he was lost again in the wandering of the Israelites, a story which particularly appealed to him.

* * *

The children stopped their shouting as Nathan Knight rode up on his recently purchased black mare, swung easily out of the saddle and tossed the reins over a white-painted fence post. A small, neat school stood in its yard on the outskirts of Gila City. It was so neat and pretty that Nathan wished with all of his heart he could have gone to a school just as this to learn to read and write properly.

"Miss Grayson's inside. She is writin' on the blackboard," cried one of the children, while the rest gaped at the black-clad figure of Nathan in awe.

"Thank you," said Nathan, slightly embarrassed at the looks of reverence the boys were giving him. As he walked up the gravel path to the school door he was further embarrassed when he heard one of the older girls say to her companion in a carrying whisper: "I wonder when Miss Victoria is going to marry him?"

"I reckon it's a right shame, a schoolteacher throwing herself away on a gunfighter like him," said the other girl in an equally penetrating whisper. "They say that that awful Fortune woman is keen on him too, but my Ma won't let me mention her name at home."

In the classroom, Nathan saw Victoria busy writing up the next day's lesson.

"How do, Miss Victoria," Nathan said. "I was just passin' by an' – an' I thought I'd drop in."

"It's nice to see you again, Knight," she answered. "I was just going out to get some flowers for nature study. Would you care to come along?"

Nathan discovered that he would and a few minutes later he and Victoria, with a dozen children straggling behind them, left the schoolhouse and began walking over the rough country that stretched away as far as the eye could see in search of wild flowers.

"Did you read that tract I gave you on the Evils of Drink?" asked Victoria, as they wandered along.

"Er – not all that thoroughly, miss. Fact is I'm – er, not what you might call a drinkin' man."

"No," she said. "But the place where you work supplies hard liquor to its customers. I was hoping this tract would make you realise how the Wheel of Fortune, and similar saloons, is degrading to the men of this city."

Nathan trudged on in silence, not wishing to admit that even if he had wanted to read the tract – which he had not – he would have had a great deal of difficulty in spelling out a lot of the words.

"Over the last few days since you have been coming here," continued the schoolteacher, "I have come to realise that you are not quite as I first considered you. And it seems a great shame to me that you spoil yourself by working in that terrible Wheel of Fortune place. Surely for a young man like you there are many more honest jobs in which you could employ yourself?"

"Maybe," said Nathan, "but I guess they

91

wouldn't pay the same sort of wages as I get at the Wheel."

"Money is not everything," said Victoria. "Love of money is the root of all evil."

"You're givin' me another lecture today," remarked Nathan with a sudden grin. "I reckon you're kinda wasted teachin' school. You should be in a tent giving the sinners a helpin' of hellfire and doom."

Victoria laughed. "You're quite right, Nathan," she said. "My father was a preacher and I think a lot of him has worked off on me. It's a wonder you still want to come and see me when I keep playing the part of an evangelist."

"Oh, I enjoy your company," Nathan murmured, "an' it's mighty flatterin' that you want to save my soul from the bottomless pit."

For a while they walked in silence, the children watching the two figures of the adults with keen concentration. The sombre black clothes of the young man were a contrast to the pale blue muslin of the girl's gown.

"I bet you a cent he's gonna kiss her," said one small boy to another.

"Bet he ain't," said his friend. "They'll wait till we're gone home before they do that."

"I do wish you wouldn't wear that gun when you come to visit us," said Victoria abruptly. "I don't like to see instruments of destruction around the schoolhouse. I'm sure it isn't good for my pupils."

"Beg pardon, miss, but I couldn't go out without it now. For the last few days a gun seems to have become part of me. A gun itself ain't a bad thing. It's just the way that it's used."

"In other words, it's the tool of your trade," said Victoria acidly.

"I guess you could say that," said Nathan and he carried on walking in silence, his eyes gazing into the cobalt sky above.

"Here, children," cried Victoria, pointing to the sharp leaves of a yucca. It had a large stalk on which grew white bell-shaped flowers. "Can anybody tell me what this plant is?"

"It's a Spanish Dagger, miss," cried one of the boys.

"Now what can you tell me about this?" continued Victoria.

"Please, miss, please, miss," cried several of the children.

"Yes, Dean?" she said to one of them.

"Well, miss, if you get a bite from a rattler what you do is take the leaves and stick 'em into yourself where the snake bit you and that'll cure the poison."

"Quite right," said Victoria.

From the shade of a Joshua tree, Nathan watched while Victoria continued to talk to the children about the various plants growing in the vicinity. As he watched her standing there in her neat dress that in no way disguised the youthful curves of her figure, he had to admit to himself he found a strange satisfaction in being in her presence, even though she seemed more interested in his reformation than in himself. No doubt she had taken after her father who was a preacher, but Nathan also remembered how she had helped him when he had been hiding in the arroyo. Most of the time he did not bother to take her admonishments seriously. For him

93

it was enough merely to be in her presence, and feel awaking inside him emotions and instincts that he had never dreamed of at Red Buttes. The strange thing was that he had felt exactly the same way when he was with Fortune Sarrat at the Wheel of Fortune saloon. The fact that two such opposite women could arouse the same feeling in him vaguely worried Nathan. At the back of his mind he knew he would welcome the day when he would ride off with Hannibal Reno. Women were fine. They were pretty, they were exciting. They were aggravating and often selfish and very, very changeable. All of which added up to a pretty tantalising mixture. Yet Nathan felt they were out of place in his life. He knew that there was man's work ahead of him. Love would get in the way of this. Still, until he did ride off with Reno he could see no harm in passing time with the two most opposite women in Gila City. As he watched the children and their teacher, with his thumbs tucked comfortably into his black leather gunbelt, he saw Victoria hold up a book, saying: "Now children, sit comfortably, and I will read you a story."

With looks of eager anticipation on their faces, the children settled cross-legged while Victoria took up her position in front of them, seating herself on a time-worn stone which rose from the sand like a rock in a tawny sea.

"Once upon a time," read Victoria, "there was an enchanted palace and in it was a little boy who, though he did not know it, was really a prince. Every day this little boy would stand on the battlements of the castle and look far out over the dark green forest which surrounded the castle."

Although he knew it was kids' stuff, Nathan

found himself fascinated by the unfolding of the fairy story. Subconsciously he envied these children, as apart from particularly grim excerpts from the Old Testament, he had never been read to. Victoria's voice flowed on, telling the story of the little prince, and how as he grew up he longed to get away from the magic castle and pass through the dark green forest to the wide, wide world.

Suddenly the book thudded to the ground. The teacher stifled a cry then called to one of the children in a choky voice.

"Cindy, whatever you do, do not move."

The child in question looked about her puzzled for a moment and then gave a cry of horror as she saw a large, black object crawling over her white frock. It was a large, hairy-legged desert tarantula and even the children knew it was capable of causing death.

"Keep still, Cindy," called Nathan. "The rest of you kids get back."

The child did not move. She sat as though hypnotised while the hideous insect crossed her lap and then, in an almost leaping movement, reached her forearm. Slowly it stalked the trembling flesh, then gripped the fabric of her sleeve and began to haul itself up towards the petrified child's shoulder. The other children, silent in their horror, had backed away, while Victoria had risen to her feet and was standing in an agony of indecision. She knew that if she was to attempt to beat the repulsive insect away it might bite the girl before it could be knocked off.

"Keep away from her, Victoria," Nathan ordered, as his gun hand rose steadily with the blue steel Peacemaker until it was directly in his line of vision. By now the tarantula was on the girl's shoulder. In the sights of the Colt it appeared like an obscene growth against the white outline of the girl's dress. A single trickle of sweat ran down Nathan's forehead as he aimed the gun.

His finger closed on the trigger. The gun exploded and bucked with recoil. The tarantula was plucked away from its victim and fell several yards away on the sand, a smashed monstrosity which quivered and waved its remaining legs in its death throes.

Victoria jumped forward and picked up the girl who was now screaming with hysteria. Nathan bolstered his smoking gun. A feeling of satisfaction spread through him. Not only had he saved the child with his skill as a marksman, but he had proved to Victoria that his Peacemaker had other uses than being a gunman's tool of destruction.

As they returned to the schoolhouse to the accompaniment of Cindy's sobbing, Victoria turned to Nathan, her eyes moist with gratitude.

"You don't need to say anything," Nathan said. "Maybe after this you'll understand things better. You see, the one thing I feel I can do is shoot. I ain't so good at anythin' other than that, I guess, unless you count hoein' beans."

That night in the Wheel of Fortune saloon, Fortune Sarrat gave Nathan a hard look when he strolled in to begin his night's work.

"I hear you did some pretty shooting today," she remarked coldly. "I congratulate you on that. But somehow I think your world is the saloon rather than the schoolhouse."

* * *

It was a couple of hours after the sun had

96

risen over Gila City. Already the air was trembling over the plains. Out at the diggings the miners were draining their last pannikins of coffee, rolling up their sleeves and beginning the back-breaking work of the day. In Gila City itself men walked into the hot streets and blinked in the glare. There was a jingle of harness and the shouts of the teamsters as the morning's work began. Here and there womenfolk of the town hurried along the boardwalks in their long dresses in the direction of the General Store to buy their provisions before the morning heat clamped down. At the edge of the town Victoria stood at the door of her schoolhouse and rang a bell. Obediently her class lined up, all except one little boy who could be seen in the distance running towards the school as though his life depended on it.

Red-faced and panting, he skidded into his place at the end of the line.

"Johnny Rodgers, you're late once again," Victoria chided. "It's the third bad mark you'll have got this week."

Johnny murmured something inaudible and held his head low, in anger rather than sadness. "One day," he thought, "I'll be a man. I won't need to go to school. I'll wear black clothes and ride a black horse just like Nathan Knight."

"Into school, children," said Victoria, "and don't bang your desks."

* * *

In the town jail Marshal Matt Hollis inserted a key into the lock of the lock-up door.

"How're you feeling this morning, Jim?" he asked the solitary prisoner.

"My head feels like it had a couple of wild cats

97

fightin' in it," moaned the man lying on the bunk.

"That'll teach you to be drunk and disorderly," said the marshal. "It'll be a five-dollar fine. You can stay here longer if you want to sleep it off a bit."

"Thanks, Marshal. If you could throw some coffee in with that offer I'd be mighty grateful."

In his room Hannibal Reno climbed out of bed and began pacing up and down the floor, spelling out a letter as he walked. The contents brought a slight smile of satisfaction to his harsh features. As he walked he was conscious that his limp had nearly gone.

In the room next door Nathan Knight slept peacefully. His sleep was suddenly disturbed by an urgent hammering on the door.

"What is it?" he murmured, his eyes still closed.

"Nathan, Nathan, let me in. It's Fortune," came an urgent voice. "I think there's something wrong at the Wheel."

"Just a minute, miss," called Nathan, rubbing his eyes and fighting to regain consciousness. "Just hold on a mite and I'll let you in."

He jumped out of bed, pulled on a pair of levis, and, running his fingers through his tousled hair, he lurched to the door and opened it.

"What's the matter, miss?" he asked as Fortune entered.

"I think there's something wrong at the Wheel," she repeated.

"Why, miss, what's happened? Isn't Jonas on guard?" Jonas was Fortune's black handyman who spent the early morning, when the Wheel had closed down, guarding the place with his shotgun.

"I don't know," she said, "but usually, when I go down to the Wheel, the door is open and Jonas is loafing there. As I went down now to check last night's takings, I saw it was still shut up. I just felt there was something wrong. I've never known Jonas not to have opened up and be lounging against the doorway yet. I just feel in my bones there's something wrong."

"Okay, miss," said Nathan. "Probably the lazy ol' coot is still asleep. Let's go and see."

Without waiting to put on his socks he tugged on his boots and strapped on his gunbelt. Then he banged on the wall and called out: "Hey, Reno, Miss Fortune figures there might be a bit of trouble up at the Wheel. I just thought I'd let you know in case I need help."

Next moment they were running down the street towards the Wheel of Fortune. Turning^ a corner Nathan saw a wooden building with a huge sign painted across the false front. As Fortune had said, the doors were still closed, and the shuttered windows gave it a strange blank air.

"Probably ain't nothin', miss," Nathan muttered, but he still loosened his gun in its holster. Next moment there came the roar of an explosion. Part of the roof at the rear seemed to sail in the sky before it was hidden by a rolling cloud of black smoke. There was a tremendous crash and tinkle of glass as windows were blown out. Following this, there was a moment of silence, then confusion broke out.

"Get back!" Nathan yelled to Fortune. "Someone's blowed your strongbox." Next he was racing forward, gun in hand, towards the saloon which was now almost hidden by smoke. Through this he saw dimly several figures burst from the side entrance of the building and race towards horses which had been plunging in terror at the hitching rail. Behind him he could hear the shouts of the people who had come running to see the cause of the explosion.

These shouts turned to screams as the men swung into their saddles and rode thundering down the street, firing at random as they went.

Half blinded by the smoke and dust, Nathan fired into the group as it, swept past him, turning and emptying his gun after them before they were lost to sight round the corner of a grain store.

Swinging out the cylinder of the Peacemaker to reload, he was conscious of Fortune beside him.

"Reno and I'll get after 'em," he cried.

"We'd better go and see what happened to Jonas first," she said and, grabbing him by the hand half-dragged him into the smoky interior of the Wheel of Fortune Saloon.

CHAPTER EIGHT

Inside the wrecked saloon Nathan nearly tripped over the bound form of Jonas.

"Glory be, Mister Knight," he said in a quavering voice. "Ah sure done think Ah was a-headin' for them golden stairs when dat blast went off."

"What happened, Jonas?" asked Fortune while Nathan untied him.

"Ah opened the door after sun-up like Ah allus do when a gun was pressed against my pore heart," he said excitedly. "There was several of 'em, missy, with kerchiefs round their faces. But one I recognised – Eli Hawkins."

"Charley Donohue's pal."

"Dat's right. After they done tied me up like a market chicken, Eli took 'em to your strongbox, missy. The next thing Ah know they come runnin' out of yore office an' then there was dat big explosion. Ah guess one got hurt in it – there was a mighty powerful scream."

Nathan left him and entered the short passage which led to the smouldering wreck of Fortune's office. Amid the debris lay the huddled form of a man. His flesh was blackened and blood trickled from his nose and mouth. His clothes had been partially burned in the blast and he lay on the floor in an unnatural position. Looking closely, Nathan saw that it was Eli Hawkins.

"Help me," the injured man moaned. "I feel

somethin' terrible has happened to me."

"I'll get Doc Williams if you'll tell me who led the raid," Nathan said, kneeling down beside him.

Eli Hawkins did not argue. He knew he was running out of time.

"It was Chet Webb and his boys," he murmured. "The idea to blow the strong box here came from Charley Donohue. He was tellin' us about it after Fortune had fired him. After Charley was killed I went to Chet with the idea."

"Who is this Chet Webb?" demanded Nathan.

"He runs the Webb gang," explained Fortune from behind. "They usually specialise in stage hold-ups. They're all coldblooded killers."

"They're goddamn sons of bitches," gasped the injured man.

"They left me here to die."

"Where they headin' for after they'd got the money?"

"We – they – planned to ride south to the Yellow River and then into Mexico. After the blast they didn't bother about me, they just left me lyin' here. They ran into the room, picked up the money and vamoosed. Goddamn 'em to hell."

His face twisted in agony.

"Mister, you promised to get me a doc and I've told you all

I know." "I guess Doc Williams'll be here any minute," said Fortune

soothingly.

"Better get after the Webb boys," Nathan said. "I'm kinda hopin' Mister Reno will come with me."

He glanced through the wall of the office

which had been completely shattered by the explosion. Curtains were still smouldering and in the centre of the floor was a twisted metal shape, all that remained of Fortune's strongbox Most of the smoke had now dispersed through the broken windows, and in the morning sunlight Nathan saw flashes of silver where the light caught coins which the Webb gang had overlooked in their haste.

"How much was there in that box before they blew it up?" asked Nathan.

"Between six and seven thousand dollars," replied Fortune, her voice trembling at the thought of her loss. "Every cent I'd managed to save was in that box 'cause I don't trust banks,"

"I know," murmured Nathan. "There don't seem to be anything much you can trust."

"Get me a doc, mister, get me a doc," Hawkins begged from the floor. "I done what you asked, now you gotta help me."

At that moment several figures entered the passage, Doctor Williams, Marshal Hollis and Hannibal Reno.

"Let's be goin' after them, Reno," said Nathan. "This singed coyote here tells me they'll be taking the trail down to Mexico."

"Now hold on a minute," said the marshal. "I guess it's my job to be chasin' these varmints. But I'd sure appreciate it if you came along with me. Raise your right hand and I'll swear you in as temporary deputies. That'll make it all nice and legal." A few moments later, the marshal and his new deputies left the scarred saloon and thrust their way through the crowd towards the town corral for their horses. Just as Nathan was about to swing into the saddle he saw Fortune.

"Don't you worry, miss," he said. "We'll get your money back for you."

"I'm coming to help you get it," she retorted.

"Don't be crazy, Miss Fortune," said Nathan. "It's gonna be a hard ride and there's gonna be shootin'."

"I can ride as hard as you," said Fortune. "And I don't exactly faint at the sound of gunfire."

"Now listen, miss..." began Hollis. He was interrupted by his regular deputy running up.

"Get your cayuse," barked the marshal. "We ain't got a minute to lose. They must be several miles away by now."

"Oh no, they ain't, marshal," said the deputy. "They've holed up in the schoolroom."

"What d'you mean?" the marshal demanded. "They only rode as far as the schoolhouse. They're holed up there, with all the kids and Miss Victoria."

"Gawd," breathed the marshal. "Why in the name of hell did they do a thing like that?"

"There was some shootin' when they left the Wheel of Fortune," the deputy explained. "I heard tell that Chet's brother, Austin, stopped a slug in the chest. He fell off his horse as they were goin' by the schoolhouse and Chet wouldn't leave him. Come over right away, Marshal. There's a ring of people round that schoolhouse already. If anyone is loco enough to start firin', they might hit some of the kids."

Nathan spurred his horse, causing it to plunge momentarily before speeding off through the dirt streets in the direction of the schoolhouse. Reno and Hollis raced beside him. They pulled up in a cloud of

104

dust about a couple of hundred yards in front of the schoolhouse where a silent crowd of townsfolk looked towards the white-painted building. It seemed very peaceful, the only sign of life being the outlaws' horses tied to the picket fence.

A man looked up at the marshal.

"Hollis," he said hoarsely, "My boy and daughter are in that school. We've got to save them even if it means giving those bastards safe passage and lettin' 'em keep the money."

"That's right," cried a white-faced woman. "Let them take the goddamned money but leave us our children."

"It's all the fault of that woman Fortune," cried another mother hysterically. "She's brought bad luck to this town..."

"It's her, money or our kids," came another voice.

"Why won't she let 'em keep it and save our children?" cried another. "She thinks more of her goddamned money ..."

"You're being very stupid," came the cool voice of Fortune. Nathan turned in his saddle and saw her astride her horse.

"You are angry so you turn on me," she continued. "Well, let me tell you the Webb gang are welcome to my money if they'll leave the school. But how are we to convince them of that? Being so treacherous themselves they'll never believe us. Try and parley with them, Nathan. You've got a pretty big interest in what goes on in that schoolhouse," she added acidly. "Better leave your gunbelt here and carry a flag of truce."

"If you say so, miss," said Nathan.

105

Reluctantly he unbuckled his gun and handed it to her. Then, holding a white scarf she had given him, he urged his horse forward towards the silent schoolhouse. As he came closer he became aware of a rifle barrel at one of the windows, covering his approach.

"I ain't armed," he yelled. "I've come to parley." The door of the schoolhouse swung open and a tall man appeared with a rifle.

"You Chet Webb?" shouted Nathan.

"I am," said the man. "And you're the bastard who shot my brother this mornin'."

"I've come to do a deal with you."

"The Webb gang never does deals."

He raised his rifle. There was a spurt of flame and the bullet from the Winchester plucked away the white scarf from Nathan's hand.

"The next one will be through your head."

"Don't be a blamed fool," shouted Nathan. "If you leave the schoolhouse we'll give you safe passage and you can have the doctor to look after Austin."

"Austin don't need no doctor," replied Chet. "He's past needin' one."

He pumped the lever of the rifle meaningfully. Nathan turned and cantered back. By now scores of men, taking up positions at corners and behind wagons, were covering the schoolhouse with an assortment of weapons ranging from old shotguns to the latest repeaters.

"Now don't anybody shoot," Marshal Hollis was shouting. "Whatever happens, don't shoot. You may hit one of the kids.'"

"I'm sorry," said Nathan, pulling up beside Fortune. "He just wouldn't listen to me."

106

She nodded.

"I should have gone," she said. "Perhaps they'll listen to a woman."

She touched the flank of her horse with her quirt, riding out into the open. Immediately there was the crash of a gun and a bullet whined above her head.

"Come back, miss," Hollis shouted. "The Webbs wouldn't stop at shootin' a woman."

Expertly Fortune turned her plunging steed and rode back to the shelter of a shack where Nathan and Reno were waiting for her.

"They must be loco," said Fortune angrily. "We go to offer them safe passage and they don't listen. What's wrong with them?"

"I guess they don't trust us," said the marshal. "I reckon they figure – quite rightly – that the townsfolk are pretty sore because they're holed up in the school. I've heard a lot about the Webb gang. They don't give favours and they don't expect any."

"I don't mind if I never see any of that money again," said Fortune, "as long as the children are left safe. But surely there must be something we can do?"

She turned to Reno. A slightly contemptuous look played on her face despite her anxiety.

"You've had a lot of experience of gun fighting. Can't you suggest anything?"

"I can't suggest anythin' to do with gun fighting," said Reno. "As the Webb gang is in that schoolhouse, to do anythin' with a gun would be signing a death warrant for them kids. They've got to be persuaded to leave."

"But we've tried that," said Fortune desperately.

107

"Maybe it was the wrong man?" said a worried-looking bystander. "They probably knew that Knight was Fortune's gunslinger, so they wouldn't expect a straight deal from him. Or from Fortune, seeing that she had lost the money. The deal has got to be made by somebody they could trust."

"Well, I guess there ain't anybody they would trust around here except . . . maybe . . ." a shrewd look came into his eyes. "How about Brother Paul?"

"He sure looks the part," said Fortune. "Providing he's sober. The gang might listen to him."

"Who is he?" asked Reno.

Hollis said, "He was a preacher until he took to the bottle for inspiration. But it inspired him too much, an' he could hardly condemn the Demon Drink when he was liquored up to his eyeballs. I don't know which band of religion he was affiliated to, but now he's a sorta freelance. He still sermonises sometimes an' when he ain't laid up with his little weakness, he's quite a good *hombre*. He's sure been a good friend to the miners at times. Go and get him." He nodded to his deputy who ran off.

Now an uneasy silence had fallen round the schoolhouse. The mothers of the trapped children were too tense to cry aloud. Their menfolk squinted at its frame walls over the barrels of their guns. Gun barrels became almost too hot to handle. The hot morning wore on. Having to stand in the full glare of the sun without any shade made the heads of the Webb gang's horses droop lower and lower.

At length the dour deputy returned with a shabbily dressed man with greying hair down to his shoulders. His face was pale and his eyes bloodshot. His hand shook slightly as Matt Hollis greeted him with unaccustomed warmth.

"Brother Paul, I'm mighty glad to see you here at this moment," he said. "Gila City needs you more than ever before. Being a man of the cloth, I figure if the Webb gang are gonna trust anybody it would be you. All you have to do is walk out and parley with them. I reckon if you can save the children today, you'll be remembered as long as there's a settlement in this part of the world."

The ruined preacher looked at the distant schoolhouse with his drink-bleared eyes. "You want me to walk out there an' talk to them murderers?" he asked pitifully.

The marshal nodded. "It's your big chance to put some of your words into action," he said.

A look of pain crossed the pallid features of Brother Paul. "I jest can't do it," he said hoarsely. "I can't explain it to you, but I jest can't... and anyways, what would be the use? I'd be dead before I got anywhere near the schoolhouse. I've heard of Chet Webb and his gang before. They'll kill a man as easily as some guys will light up a cigar."

The group of people, most of them parents of the schoolchildren, had begun to form around the ex-preacher. A woman stepped forward and looked him right in the face. "My Mary Lou is in that schoolhouse," she said. "You remember her, Brother Paul? That little girl with the yellow hair.

109

She wore a blue ribbon when she come to your old meetin's. You was mighty full of spit and confidence then. Damning us all to hell-fire, telling us to repent. Now it's our turn to tell you to be a man and go out there to save Mary Lou and the other kids. If you don't, if anything happens to even one of them children you'll never have a night again you can sleep through. Wherever you go people will point to you and say 'Look at him, there goes the preacher who turned his back on the kids at Gila City'."

Tears began to course down the woman's cheeks.

"I don't rightly figger what I can do, ma'am," said Brother Paul awkwardly.

"You can take a message from the townsfolk of Gila," said Marshal Hollis. "Tell them there's a free passage with the gold – " he glanced over to Fortune and she nodded, "As far as, say, Yellow River, in return for them quitting the schoolhouse and leaving all the kids behind."

With the agony of fear written on his face, Brother Paul looked again towards the schoolhouse. "It's such a long way to walk, knowing there's guns trained on you which any second may blast you into damnation."

"Let me have a word with you, preacher," said Hannibal Reno gently.

The small crowd moved back as Hannibal took his arm and walked away out of earshot. The spectators saw that Hannibal Reno spoke rapidly to the preacher. At the same time he drew a flask from his pocket and proffered it to him. Gratefully he seized it and put it to his lips. A minute later

110

Reno's lips stopped moving. The preacher nodded his head and the two men returned.

"It's all right," said Reno. "The preacher here is going out there to parley with Chet. Ain't that so?"

Brother Paul nodded, his face sheened with the sweat of fear.

"Yes," he murmured. "I'll go. Tell me again what I've got to say to them, if they'll even listen."

As Matt Hollis explained, someone gave the preacher a white cloth tied to a stick.

"May the Lord have mercy on me," he faltered and walked out into the open.

Everyone watched with baited breath as he walked towards the schoolhouse. Once or twice he paused irresolutely, then carried on. When he reached the low playground fence he seemed to have difficulty in opening the gate. At last it was open and he walked through towards the school door.

"What did you say to him, Reno?" Nathan whispered with curiosity.

Reno, who had been watching the progress of the preacher through his tinted spectacles, smiled slightly.

"I just reminded him of a few things," he said. "I guess there comes a time in a lot of men's lives when all they need is a little remindin'. I guess if he comes through this all right, he won't need to punish himself so hard."

The door of the schoolhouse opened to the preacher's knock. He entered and it closed again. A universal sigh rose from the onlookers.

Minutes dragged by, then the door opened again. Brother Paul came out and began running across the open ground. It was soon discernible to all that his face, which a few minutes ago had been strained by his hangover and his fear, was now jubilant.

"Agreed, they've agreed," he cried in delight. "Chet Webb says they accept a safe passage to Yellow River on condition that his brother Austin gets a proper burial at Boothill. They'll let the children come out and then they'll ride off. If it's acceptable to you, Marshal, they want you to fire just one shot into the air."

Matt Hollis drew his Colt and signalled his agreement.

For several minutes nothing happened, then children streamed out of the schoolhouse and began running towards their parents who waited for them with arms outstretched.

"I guess there's a parcel of folks here who owe you a deep debt of gratitude, preacher," said Matt Hollis, "You've just done a mighty fine thing, especially as you were scared."

Without a word the preacher turned towards Reno.

"Thanks, Reno," he said at length and walked away quickly into Gila City.

The joyous shouts of the children died away and when the last toddler was clear of the schoolhouse, an expectant silence fell. All eyes were riveted on the door, waiting to see Chet and his henchmen leave. Not far away Nathan heard the snick of a rifle bolt. Marshal Hollis heard it too and called out: "Remember, folks, I promised them free passage."

"You may have done, Marshal," said the man with the rifle, "but I don't believe in dealin' with varmints like that. The first one to come through that door is going to get a bellyful of lead. What's the point of giving them a free passage when we could mow 'em down?"

"Victoria Grayson is still in that schoolhouse," snapped Nathan. "Down your rifle or I'll bust you over the head..."

His words were interrupted by a whip-like command from Marshal Hollis to his deputy. "Arrest that man," he said. "I ain't gonna let anyone here break the word that we gave, though personally I hope they fry in hell once they're across the Yellow River."

The next moment a small gang left the schoolhouse and walked to their tethered mounts. As they did so, a gasp of consternation went up from the onlookers. In the centre of the group they could see the sun gleaming on the golden hair of Victoria Grayson. Next moment she climbed into the saddle of one of the horses. The outlaws surrounded her and the small cavalcade jingled out of the school yard, heading in an easterly direction across the plain.

"Come on, Reno," said Nathan. "We've got to trail them sons-of-bitches."

Reno nodded. Just as Nathan was climbing into the saddle of his black mare, a tall broad-shouldered man with a curly blond beard came and looked up at him.

"I'd take it kindly as a favour if I could come along with you," he said. "I feel I owe it to

113

you, Knight. Ever since you shot that there desert spider off my Cindy's arm."

"If you can use a shootin' iron we'll be glad to have you along," said Nathan. "Them critturs are sure gonna pay for breakin' their word and taking Miss Victoria along as hostage."

As the men were getting ready to follow the departed Webb gang, Fortune rode up to Nathan.

"I'm coming too," she said.

"Don't be silly," said Nathan. "It ain't no work for a woman."

She looked at him coldly. "You don't know me, Knight," she said. "Remember I was a border child. I bet I can use a gun dam' near as well as you. And you sure need a woman along if you manage to get the schoolmarm away from those men."

"It's just that I guess it's gonna be pretty dangerous. There's gonna be a lot o' lead flying once we hit the Yellow River."

Fortune lit one of her long black cheroots, and blew the smoke into Nathan's face. "Don't forget you're the hired hand," she said. "After all, it's my gold in their saddle-bags."

CHAPTER NINE

The Yellow River was aptly named. Like a clay-coloured snake it wound through a semi-desert wilderness. Through countless centuries, its sluggish waters had gouged out a bed so deep that for a thirsty traveller on the inhospitable plain an attempt to reach water involved a perilous descent. Here and there the level of the plain dipped and then, for a brief space, the Yellow River had the level banks of more conventional rivers. The few trails that crossed the wilderness became fords at such places, and it was to such a ford that Chet Webb was leading his small band. Beyond the river they knew lay safety and a chance to spend the money stolen from the Wheel of Fortune in the drinking houses and bordellos of Mexico. Here too ended the safe passage guaranteed by Matt Hollis, but this did not cause them a moment's worry. The promise had only been of value in getting them clear of Gila City. If a posse did have the courage to follow them beyond the Yellow River, they still had a trump card in the form of their pretty hostage.

The gang had been riding hard through the hot day, and now as evening approached Chet turned to his men.

"Guess we'll make camp at Crazy Steer ford," he growled. "We'll cross over ol' Yellow tomorrow mornin'."

"In that case we'll still be safe from any Gila City sons-of-bitches tonight," laughed a grizzled man named Hansen who, now Austin had been shot, had become Chet's second-in-command.

He turned to the drooping figure of Victoria Grayson. Her hands were still tied behind her back, and her skin was burned red from the fierce rays of the desert sun.

"I hope you won't mind sleepin' rough tonight, lady," he said in a sneering voice. "Still, I guess the charmin' company of Chet an' the boys will more than make up for it. Perhaps you'll find their manners to be a little peculiar, but that's 'cause they ain't had the company of womenfolk for some time. I guess you'll soon get used to their ways."

A sob broke, from the parched throat of the girl

"You are safely away now," she cried above the soft sound of the horses' hooves on the coarse soil. "Please turn me loose."

"Ah, we couldn't do that, ma'am," Hansen grinned sardonically. "Like I said, the boys ain't had no womenfolk company for a mighty long time, an' they're sorta looking to you ..."

Several miles back along the trail another small group cantered steadily, a plume of dust hanging in the warm air behind them. At the head of it rode Marshal Matt Hollis and Hannibal Reno. Though Hollis was glad to have an expert gunfighter like Reno with him, he had not altered his opinion of bounty hunters. Equally Reno had no desire to talk. He continuously scanned the trail ahead through his tinted spectacles. At length the party reined up to rest their foam-flecked mounts.

"I reckon they'll probably spend the night at Crazy Steer ford," said Cindy's father, Eddie Frost.

116

"You could be right," grunted Hollis. "I reckon they'll need to rest their cayuses after ridin' all day. 'Sides, they'd still be in the safe passage area ..."

"You can't still give them safe passage," said Nathan from where he stood beside Fortune. "Not after they kidnapped Victoria."

"Yeah, I reckon so," said the marshal. "I figure a good place to jump anybody is when they're tryin' to cross a ford."

"What about Victoria?" said Fortune. "Have any of you bright sparks figured out how you're gonna get her away before the lead starts to fly."

"We might over-run them when they're asleep," Nathan said. "Maybe we could hustle her off in the confusion."

"They'd have sentries, don't you worry," said Hollis. "They are a mighty professional bunch. And mighty ruthless too. If they saw Miss Victoria being taken off any one of the gang would put a bullet in her back just for the hell of it."

"C'mon, let's hit the trail," Reno said. "We don't want them to know we are after them, but we don't want them too far ahead either."

The posse, which totalled eight including Fortune in her dust powdered riding habit, swung back into their saddles and continued along the trail. In places it was lined by the sightless skulls of steers who had been the victims of a disastrous attempt to drive a herd south from Gila City, to an Indian reservation far beyond the Yellow River.

As dusk gathered the mounts began to labour up a steep slope. When at last they reached the top of the ridge the riders could just make out the dark

117

curves of the river as it twisted across the darkening plain.

Hollis raised an army telescope and then lowered it with satisfaction.

"Like you said, Eddie, they're campin' close to the ford," he said.

"What are we going to do now?" asked Fortune.

"I guess we'll follow their example," Hollis replied. "Let's move back out of their line of sight an' then we'll brew up some coffee."

* * *

Victoria Grayson sat in the glow of a small fire made from mesquite stacks. Her hands had been untied while she had been allowed to eat a plateful of beans and drink a mug of coffee, but now they were bound again. Her wrists were paining from the cruel bite of the cord.

She looked fearfully at the stark, stubbled faces of the Webb gang which she could see etched in the dramatic light of the fire. Chet sat a little apart from the others, gazing into the embers with a strange brooding expression on his features. The rest were in a semi-circle. A bottle of Red Eye was passing from hand to hand. Hansen seemed to be in high spirits, perhaps because of the quantity of raw spirit which had burned its way down his gullet, or perhaps because of the feeling of power he held over the bound schoolmistress.

"When are we gonna share out the dollars, Chet?" cried one of the men.

"I reckon when we hit Jolita will be soon enough," the leader answered in low tones.

"Waal, we've got more than dollars to share

tonight, boys," said Hansen, leering in the direction of Victoria. "I wonder who is gonna be the lucky first."

Several of the gang sniggered.

"I reckon it's gonna be rather special, gettin' to know a schoolmarm," he went on. "I allus figured they were different to ordinary women... I remember my schoolmarm when I was a kid. Every day she used to lay a rod across my back cause she reckoned I was stupid. I sure learned to hate the breed. But I got even, I burned down that goddamn schoolhouse the night I quit home. Blazed up nice an' pretty."

He paused to take another gulp at the bottle.

"'Course that schoolmarm didn't look at all like Miss Victoria here. She was like an old fowl at the end of a hard winter. But Miss Victoria – waal, now, I reckon she ain't had time to grow into lookin' like a regular sour-cat schoolmarm. An' I reckon after she has got to know us boys she won't be no more interested in her classroom."

Victoria lowered her head to her knees and tried to stop her tears. She was terrified. There was not one man there who she could appeal to. Oh, why hadn't someone come after them to save her? Where was Nathan Knight? He could certainly shoot. She remembered the way he had shot the tarantula off the trembling Cindy.

Hansen stood up, slightly unsteady in the firelight. In the background the tethered horses moved slightly and the sentry, sitting a little distance away on a flat-topped rock with a rifle across his knees, hummed "Streets of Laredo" monotonously. The full moon was just hoisting itself above the horizon and its silver light began to

119

shrink the shadows.

"It's sure a nice night," Hansen mused. "Reckon it's a shame for you to be trussed up like some old chicken." He walked over and bent over Victoria. His knife flashed briefly in the new moonlight. Victoria felt a fresh stab of pain as the blade sawed at the cord, then her bonds fell away. Grabbing her by the arm, Hansen swung her up to her feet.

"Reckon we oughta be sociable," he grinned. "Come on, Miss Victoria, let's have a dance. The boys will sing us a tune.. come on fellas, give us 'Buffalo Gals.'"

"Please, do not touch me," gasped the girl, struggling as the outlaw's arms tightened around her.

"I'll teach you to be so durned high an' mighty," Hansen snarled. With hunger his mouth sought hers.

"Goddamn you, Hansen, let that gal be." The voice was low and deadly. Normally nothing would have stopped Hansen now, nothing but the voice of Chet Webb. It was the one thing he feared, and it cut through his lust like a cold blade.

His arms dropped to his side.

"Aw, Chet, I was jest havin' a bit of fun."

"Austin's hardly cold, an' you are messin' about with that blamed gal. You forget I lost a fine brother today. How can I think of him with you varmints gettin' drunk an' thinkin' you're a bunch of hell-raisers jest cause you got a gal on your hands. You makes me sick. An' you know how I get when I feel sick . . ." There was silence.

"Sorry, Chet," muttered Hansen.

Victoria sank back by the fire. No one

thought of tying her hands again.

* * *

In the glow of a small fire on the slope of the protecting ridge the posse sat cross-legged with tin plates of bacon and beans before them. Fortune was pouring out coffee.

"Reckon we may as well turn in early," the marshal remarked. "It's gonna be a hard, sore day tomorrow."

"So you still reckon on attacking them while they cross the ford," said Fortune, handing a steaming mug to Nathan. Hollis nodded. "Surely, if you do that it will put that schoolteacher girl in great danger."

"Can you suggest anything better, miss?" he asked.

"Perhaps they'll let her go once they are across the Yellow River."

"Not a hope, miss. We'll jest have to try and do it careful. If we get up on the bluffs we maybe'll be able to pick off the nearest guys to her as they swim the hosses across. I heard tell you are pretty handy with a rifle," he said turning to Nathan. "It'll be your job to drop the guy who will be leadin' Miss Grayson's horse."

Nathan looked down at the new Sharps rifle resting beside him. It was a fine weapon, which he had bought with his earnings from the Wheel of Fortune, and with which he had been secretly practising out of earshot of Gila City on his off-hours.

"Reckon I can give it a try," he murmured.

"You'd better not miss, Knight," said Fortune. "I guess you would be the cause of

Victoria's death if you don't shoot the man with her right away ..."

Nathan compressed his lips tight, but said nothing. Having gulped his coffee, he laid the rifle across his knees and began oiling the breech mechanism.

"Reckon you're goin' about it the wrong way," Reno remarked, standing up in the fire glow. "That girl Grayson won't have a chance in the middle of a gun battle. Why, she'll be bound on her hoss, so even if she doesn't get a bullet from one of the Webb gang, she'll probably drown in the river."

Matt Hollis looked up at the tall bounty hunter with dislike.

"You got a better idea, Reno?" he demanded.

"I'm gonna get the girl away tonight," announced Reno. "You comin' along with me?" he asked, looking down at Nathan who was engrossed with his rifle.

"Sure," he replied. He put the cap back on his oil bottle. "Now listen here," said the marshal. "This is my posse. I'm the marshal, and you're my sworn deputies, so remember what I say goes. There ain't gonna be no night raid on the Webb mob. Understand?"

"I ain't talkin' about a raid," said Reno. "I was talkin' about gettin' Victoria Grayson away."

"It'd come to the same thing. An' most of the gang would probably get away in the dark. Nope, we've got to nail them when they cross ol' Yellow. I guess you're thinkin' there'll be more chance of recoverin' the loot your way. Mebbe you're scared it will go to the bottom of Crazy Steer ford if we wait until mornin'.."

The others looked hard at Reno to see how he would take the gibe. He remained calm and his voice was low when he said: "I guess you don't like me much, Marshal."

"That's about the size of it," said the Marshal. "I ain't never had no time for bounty huntin', for men who live off blood money – though I will allow that by all accounts you are a handy shot, an' for that reason I'm glad to have you here." As he had been speaking Matt Hollis hoisted himself to his feet, and now the two men faced each other across the small fire.

"It won't do no, good for us to fall out," the marshal continued. "So, as my deputy, jest carry on an' do what I say. I'm a lawfully elected marshal and my word is the law here. It's gotta be that way."

"I reckon Mister Hollis is right," chimed in his tall, dour deputy.

"I'll tell you somethin' for nothin', Marshal," Reno said almost pensively. "For once I wasn't thinking of the money. I was thinkin' about a girl held by the Webb boys. I reckon come sun-up she might not be all that glad to be alive. The Webbs are rough with womenfolk. I guess you must have heard tell about what they done to that homesteader's wife over Caleb County way. They reckon when she was found afterwards she was loco ..."

"Maybe he's right," said Fortune. "When I think of that poor girl down there, even though

123

she used to be stuck up and prissy, I feel nothing but pity – and anger against those beasts. Reno is right."

"I tell you it wouldn't work," Hollis almost shouted. "It's a crazy idea."

"I guess you may be sayin' it because it's my notion, not because you really think it a bad plan," Reno drawled. "But it don't matter, cause Nathan an' me are goin'"

"You stay where you are," snapped the Marshall. Nathan saw that his hand was resting on his gun butt.

Reno shook his head.

"You damn well do as I say, you lousy, scalp-huntin' son-of-a-bitch." Hollis made to draw his gun, but with a swift sweep of his arm, Reno's fist pistoned against his jaw. He reeled back. Reno leapt after him through the smoky glow of the fire and again his large fist smashed against the head of the lawman.

Dazed by the impact of the blows, Hollis fell back, stumbled and fell flat on his back. His eyes were on the dark figure of Reno, and from his prone position he painfully raised his gun.

Nathan leapt forward and kicked it spinning from his hand.

"Do that an' you'll warn Webb," he said.

Hollis sat up, wiping his face with his hand.

"One of these days you are sure gonna pay for what you done," he said. "Sooner or later guys like you fall foul of the law, Reno, because it's in your mean, greedy natures, and then I'm gonna see that you gets what's comin' to you personal."

"Hasta la vista," Reno said. "The moon is

comin' up, so we can see our way. We'll have to go on foot."

* * *

Floods of silver light poured down from the great disc of the moon sailing over the edge of the dark world. It cast weird shadows and turned the deep course of the Yellow River into an inky black gash across the face of the plain. Near the Crazy Steer ford the members of the Webb gang slept on their slickers close to the fire. Some little distance away Victoria Grayson lay rolled in a horse blanket, almost too fearful to go to sleep and yet tortured by the need to close her eyes and slip into temporary forgetfulness.

On a rock above the figures sat a guard, his rifle resting across his knees, his eyes wandering over the ghostly plain and ever returning to the restless picket line of horses. In his cupped hand he held a cigarette and he shivered slightly as a cool breeze swept across the plain, carrying with it the faint cry of a coyote. He was cold, and stiff from the day's ride. He hated sentry duty and was looking forward to the time when he would shake Hansen into wakefulness for his turn. Meanwhile he tried to kill time, and his own physical discomfort, by thinking what he would do with his share of the dollars which had been snatched from the safe at the Wheel of Fortune. This money now rested in Chet Webb's saddlebags,

One thing he was going to do was to go to the best tailor in Jolita and get an outfit that would knock out the eye of any senorita who happened to glance his way. He was tired of his sweaty range clothes. He and the rest of the gang had endured a long spell travelling, and now the desire for town

125

clothes – real stylish town clothes – was almost like physical hunger with him. He would also get new boots, soft Mexican tooled-leather boots with high heels and silver spurs with a silver dollar where the rowels normally fitted so that he would jingle slightly as he walked. And a new hat. A white Stetson... By Gawd, he could see himself now, swaggering along the sidewalk, pushing his way through the batwing doors of saloons, savouring the moment as the regulars turned and saw the long-barrelled Colt in his waistband and heard the whispers: "That swell-dressed hombre is Tex Bell. He rides with Chet Webb ..."

There was a slight noise near at hand. Bell shifted his rifle, and looked about him. In all directions the moonlight-lit sage moved in the chill night breeze like a restless sea. A slight anxiety filled the sentry's mind. A whole bunch of Apaches could worm up to the small encampment under cover of the grey vegetation.

He drew on his cigarette again. He must be getting jittery. At the moment the Indian tribes were peaceful. There were no war parties out, and normally the wilderness round the Yellow River was shunned. The game was poor here, apart from the turgid river there was no water, and the Indians liked above everything to camp near sweet water.

It must have been a prairie dog, Bell thought to himself. His mind returned to the pleasant thoughts of his new clothes and how he would amuse himself in Jolita. He wondered if a certain tall Mexican girl was still to be found in a house known as Juanita's Happy Place. He could not remember her name, but there were other things that sprang to mind vividly. If she was still there he'd show her a time. He'd show her

126

how a member of the Chet Webb gang could spread his dollars and take his pleasure.

It was in the midst of these thoughts that the butt of Hannibal Reno's Colt crashed against the back of his head with sickening efficiency. Tex Bell gave a deep sigh, twitched slightly and slumped forward.

Nathan helped the tall bounty hunter lift the unconscious guard from his vantage point, then Nathan took up his position, his rifle across his knees trying to imitate Bell's outline.

"Keep me covered," hissed Reno.

"Surely."

Cautiously Reno moved forward towards the huddled sleepers. Any moment one might roll over or open his eyes and see his silhouette against the moon. These outlaws slept with their guns ready for instant action. If it came to a shoot-out the two interlopers would soon lose their advantage of surprise.

Nathan watched Reno's progress with his heart hammering. Would Reno be able to *see* Victoria, or would he stumble into one of the sleeping gang? He moved his rifle barrel in the direction of the smouldering campfire, ready to fire at the slightest movement.

* * *

Victoria Grayson felt rather than saw a presence bending over her. She turned her head and looked up to see the shape of Reno, throwing her into deep shadow with his bulk. Her mouth opened wide for the scream of terror which fought for release, but before she could utter a sound a gloved hand clamped cruelly over her face and the scream emerged only as a pathetic moan,

127

"Keep quiet, Miss Victoria," Reno whispered, still keeping his large hand in place. "I've come to get you away. One sound an' all hell will bust loose. If I take my hand away, don't scream. Okay?"

The terrified girl tried to nod her head to assure him.

"Quick," he said. "We'll have to move fast. Are you tied?"

She shook her head. Holding her hand, the big man helped her to her feet.

"Follow me."

Pulling her after him, Reno bent double and ran off between patches of sage.

Nathan watched the two disappear and continued his sentry go. After five minutes he would follow. From the ground beside the rock on which he sat there came a moan from Tex Bell as he gradually began to return from the depths of his unconsciousness.

"Quiet, buddy, if you don't want me to put you down," Nathan murmured grimly to himself.

Long minutes. The wail of the lonesome coyote drifted across the plain once more. Then Nathan, gun in hand, climbed down from the rock and began running through the sage in the same direction taken by Reno and Victoria Gray son. A few minutes later he heard a vague sound from the camp. Bell was swearing wildly, holding his head and telling his friends: "That goddam schoolmarm. She musta jumped me ... musta bust me over the head with a rock. I figured she was all tied up . . ."

"You must have been asleep, damn you,"

shouted Hansen. "Fancy lettin' a gal like that make a break. You should be plumb ashamed of yourself."

"I guess you think I let it happen for fun," yelled Bell, looking at the blood on his hands from his head wound. "I suppose you think ..."

"Stow it," commanded Ghet Webb, the only man who had not bothered to rise from his slicker. "She can't get far by herself. She'll be so scairt alone out there, by mornin' she'll be back, beggin' us to take her along. Mark my words. You take over sentry go, Hansen."

A coyote call echoed eerily across the plain and Hansen gave a cruel grin.

CHAPTER TEN

Nathan shivered uncontrollably as he lay on the edge of the bluff in the cold pre-dawn darkness. He had his slicker about him in a vain endeavour to retain some warmth in his body. What worried him most was the numbness of his hands which held the Sharps buffalo gun. Without life in his hands, how would he ever be able to aim, fire and reload when the shooting began at the Crazy Steer ambush! In the East the intensity of the darkness seemed to be lessening. Soon the pale dawn light would begin to filter across the plain and Chet Webb and his gang would make ready to cross the Yellow River. Now as they lay round the cold ashes of their campfire they little dreamed of the hungry guns which were waiting for them.

Following the rescue of Victoria Grayson, Marshal Matt Hollis had outlined his plan for the ambush. To Nathan fell the task of sniping from a high bluff overlooking the clay-coloured river. As soon as his bullets threw confusion into the gang, the rest of the posse would gallop up and engage the fugitives from the bank. Reno pointed out that if Chet Webb was as smart as he was supposed to be, he would not let the gang cross in a body but would leave a rearguard on the west bank until enough of his men were safely on the east to provide a covering fire if necessary.

"It's jest a risk we'll have to take," said the marshal. "After all, he can't be that plumb alert if you an' Knight were able to snatch Miss Victoria away as you did."

"They did not think they were being followed," said Victoria Grayson timidly from where she sat beside Fortune, warming herself at the glowing embers of the posse's fire. "They were very arrogant, and I do not think they thought anyone in Gila City would have the courage to go after them."

"I guess they know better now," said Nathan. "If they had any sense they'd be on their way."

"That ford is mighty tricky," the marshal's regular deputy remarked. "They'd be plumb loco to try an' cross in the dark."

While the posse had discussed the plan, Reno sat back in the shadows without saying a word. At last Nathan turned to him.

"What do you think about it, Mister Reno?" he asked.

The bounty hunter shrugged his shoulders.

"Guess it's all we can do," he answered. "When the chips are down it won't be no plan that will get the Webb gang but plain hard shootin'." He pulled his dark slicker round his shoulders and lay down.

"I reckon we oughta get some shut-eye," Hollis said. "We'll have to take up our positions when the moon's goin' down. Chet an' his mob'll probably cross at sun up."

Now, as the east continued to lighten, Nathan squinted into the emptiness before him, his cheek resting against the icy stock of the long-barrelled .50 rifle. Soon he would have a clear view of the ford and the sloping bank which ran down to it. At the moment everything appeared as varying shades of grey, but soon colour would come to the world – the pale blue of the early morning sky, the dun-coloured plain with its splashes of olive-hued vegetation, and, more dramatically, the red and ochre walls of the Yellow River.

At the Webb gang's camp the men begin to stir and swear at the cold and the stiffness in their limbs. One man called Sayce, not aware that he would be dead within the hour, revived the small fire and began heating coffee while the man who had been doing the last spell of guard duty stamped his feet and watched with increasing impatience.

"I've seen some mighty greenhorn fire-lightin' in my life, but I guess you take first prize every time," he growled. "You ain't gettin' any heat outa that durned little flicker. It'll be noon afore that cawffee boils."

"If you can do better, you're more than welcome," Sayce snapped back. "Otherwise do me a favour an' keep your big mouth buttoned."

"Stow it, you guys," said Chet Webb. "Soon it'll be light enough to cross the Crazy Steer, so let's get coffee an' be on our way. I don't like this place much."

"There ain't no sign of that gal," Hansen told his leader. "Mebbe she's lost."

"Forget her. There'll be enough gals for you in Jolita."

"She still might have been useful as a hostage. Don't forget we're carryin' a lot of coin, Chet. There's a good reason for the law to come after us."

132

Chet snorted.

"The law. The only law in Gila was Hollis an' he's best at arrestin' drunks once they're passed out." Hansen shrugged.

"There was that guy who gunned down Austin," he said, almost afraid to remind Chet of his brother's death. "Mebbe..."

"It was a lucky shot. Quit talkin'. We're the Webb gang, ain't we. It would take more than a few stumblebums from Gila City to hunt us. It ain't the U.S. Cavalry we're speakin' about."

"Sure, Chet, sure," Hansen muttered and he went to saddle his horse.

From the top of the bluff Nathan saw a tip of pure gold appear above the horizon. The light clouds in the west seemed to suddenly reflect a rosy glory as the sun appeared, and the lone rifleman was comforted with the thought that soon its heat would roll across the wilderness and his body would cease to tremble. He moved his position slightly so that the sights of the rifle were exactly on the spot where he thought the Webb gang would enter the ford.

Where the river emerged briefly from between the steep cliffs of its course it lived up to its name as the early sunlight shone on its turgid yellow surface. There was something about it which fascinated Nathan. It was not like any body of water he had ever seen. It seemed almost solid.

Suddenly he drew in his breath. Into his line of vision trotted a small group of riders. They seemed so small, almost toy-like, as they reined up at the bank and prepared to cross. Nathan's hands opened and closed on the Sharps. His heart beat faster and he experienced a strange sick feeling in the pit of his stomach. Within seconds he would have one of those tiny dolls in his sights, he would squeeze the trigger and a human life would be blotted out. If he was lucky and his aim was good, the victim might not know what struck him. He would die without even the chance of drawing his gun and making a fight for his life.

For a moment Nathan doubted if he had been right in wanting to follow Reno... was he really cut out to be a man-hunter? Then he remembered the cold-blooded crimes of the Webb gang... the stage driver and his passengers slaughtered on the Nogales trail, the bank manager tortured to give a safe combination at Las Cruces, the wife of the homesteader left demented! They were wolves, not men. And why should he be troubled to look down his gun barrel at a wolf.

At the edge of the Crazy Steer ford two men urged their mounts forward while the rest of the gang watched from their saddles. At first the horses seemed jittery, and Nathan could imagine the riders running their spurs along their flanks to make them enter the silted water.

Tossing their heads, the mounts splashed forward. Soon they were hock-deep, then they were up to their chests. Seconds later only their heads showed above the surface.

The Sharps unerringly followed the leading rider until he was in midstream. He turned in the saddle to say something to his mate and Nathan pulled the trigger. The explosion of the 70-grain charge deafened Nathan. The echo of the report was tossed back and forth between the canyon-like walls of the river. Slowly the man called Sayce slumped forward, then rolled out of his saddle and disappeared with hardly a splash beneath the solid-seeming surface of the Yellow River.

His companion looked about wildly, not knowing whether to go back to his companions or urge his horse across to the opposite bank. Nathan hastily raised himself up so he could work the bolt of the rifle. He fed in a new cartridge and swung the gun on to the men on the bank. Already they were unsheathing their guns, wheeling on their horses and trying to locate their hidden foe.

In the confusion it was hard to get a steady target. Nathan gave up and fired into the midst of the gang. A horse reared with a whinny of pain. Next moment, in response to the signal of Nathan's shot, the posse members spurred their horses from their hiding places and galloped towards the ford with their revolvers blazing inaccurately.

The Webb gang returned the fire. No doubt obeying an order from Chet, several urged their horses into the water. By the time Nathan had reloaded the riders were in the middle of the stream while those left on the west bank continued to hold back the posse. The Sharps thundered again, but the only effect of the heavy bullet was to throw up a brief spout a yard in front of the leading rider.

Nathan cursed his aim and rapidly reloaded, but by the time he was ready to fire the first of the Webb gang were spurring their horses up the steep east bank. Here they dismounted, took up positions behind outcrops of creamy coloured rock and began covering fire for their companions who were still swapping shots with Marshal Hollis' party.

The second half of the Webb gang crossed the ford with bullets churning the water about them. They seemed to bear charmed lives despite the heavy fire, and looking down on the scene Nathan realised that the posse was firing with their handguns which had little accuracy at such a distance.

"If only I knew which was Chet," he murmured to himself as once again he swung the rifle into a direct line with a rider. Again he pulled the trigger, again there was the heavy roar of the gun which echoed along the river and rolled across the plain to die away beyond the ragged horizon. In the middle of the ford a horse reared suddenly, blood pouring from its distended nostrils. For a moment it rolled its eyes at the pitiless sky, bewildered by pain and the injustice of its fate, then it crashed back into the river where it disappeared in a welter of muddy foam. Its rider was catapulted out of the saddle. For a moment he vanished from sight, then reappeared swimming strongly. The current gripped him, whirled him round and swept him away still striking out bravely. A moment later he was out of Nathan's range of vision.

The remainder of the gang, on reaching the far bank, took up positions with their companions and sent volley after volley crashing across the ford. A pall of dark powder smoke began to hang over the water. On the west bank the pursuers had dismounted and they, too, had taken cover so that the ambush had turned into a shooting match with both sides equally pinned down.

From his vantage point, Nathan could see

the gun flashes of either party, but now that the outlaws were behind rocks he had little chance of picking any of them off. Cautiously he got to his feet and began to climb down the bluff. Once a bullet whined close to him and left a silver streak on a rockface, but he believed he was out of effective range for most weapons. By listening to the gunfire he knew that the Webb gang was armed with Winchesters. He would have been apprehensive if he had heard the boom of a Sharps similar to his.

Soon he reached the base of the bluff and began hurrying round to the trail which led to the ford. As he ran clumsily in his high-heeled boots he saw a figure lying back in the shadow of a large boulder. Fortune was bending over it. As Nathan ran up she turned and said: "A bullet's smashed his arm, but he's all right for the moment."

"Who is he?" asked Nathan between his gasps. Fortune wiped her bloodied hands. "Frost," she said. "The father of that little girl ..."

"I know," he cut her short. "Anythin' I can do?"

"Get on an' give the boys a hand," came the weak voice of the wounded man. "They sure need it."

"Be seein' you," said Nathan, preparing to run on. "Nathan," began Fortune, getting to her feet. "Yes?"

"Nathan ... take care."

"Surely," he answered with a grin. "I figure on stayin' alive a mite longer,"

"Don't joke, Nathan. I want you to know,.. oh, damn!" The reason for her annoyance was the arrival of Victoria, with a

137

water bottle, from round a shoulder of rock.

"Here you are, Mister Frost," she said. "I got it from your horse . .. oh, Nathan."

"Mornin', ma'am," said Nathan politely.

"Nathan, I never got the chance to thank you properly," the schoolteacher murmured. "This is hardly the place..." she darted a look at Fortune who had knelt down again by Frost. "But come back so I can – " Her last words were almost drowned by a crescendo of gunfire.

"Excuse me, ladies," Nathan said, "but I guess I gotta get along. It sure sounds like a war has bust out."

"Take care," cried Victoria. "Please take care."

"Perhaps I could have the water," Fortune said acidly. "At the moment Mister Frost is more in need of comfort than Nathan Knight." Victoria blushed and handed over the canteen. Nathan continued along the trail. When it rounded a large outcrop of ancient rocks he found himself in full view of the ford. Bending low he ran forward until he could discern the broad, black-garbed back of Hannibal Reno stretched out behind a dead horse. A swarm of bullets from across the river hummed about him like enraged insects, but he was still uninjured when he hurled himself flat behind the dead but still twitching animal.

"Howdy, Mister Reno," he, greeted his partner. "How's the battle goin'?"

"It ain't," Reno replied. "It's just a coupla bunches of guys lettin off lead. I guess we were too slow comin' up after that first shot of your'n. You done well. You've got two of the varmints out of the way."

"So what happens now?"

"Just wait. You've gotta have patience... like him." He pointed above his head where a distant buzzard hung suspended in the sky. "That ole crittur sure knows his time is comin', an' so he's prepared to wait. We've gotta do the same."

"But mebbe they'll get away."

Reno shook his head.

"If those fellas across there leave their cover they won't stand a bat-in-hell's chance."

There was a lull in the firing as though both sides realised the futility of wasting ammunition.

"I reckon if one could get across ol' Yellow lower down an' get behind the Webb mob there might be a chance of finishin' 'em off," said Nathan presently. "Otherwise they can stay put till nightfall an' then be on their way."

"I was kinda thinkin' the same," Reno remarked. "But it sure would be a cussed job. Once the river leaves the ford the banks are like the walls of a small canyon. Then there's the current. It's sure a powerful one. Can you swim, boy?"

Nathan shook his head.

"Our hosses would have to get us over," he said.

Across the Crazy Steer a gun crashed and a bullet "plunked" sickeningly into the carcase of the horse.

"Trouble is, no self-respectin' cayuse would ever go down the rock to the river," Reno said. "An' if it did, Gawd knows how it would get up the other side ..."

"I've got a notion, Mister Reno," Nathan

exclaimed. "If we rode in kinda fast we could get into the river here, at the ford, an' let the current carry us down out of range."

Reno looked doubtfully through his tinted spectacles at his companion. "It's the gettin' out which I figure is the big problem."

"Sure," Nathan agreed, "But a hoss wants to stay alive as much as a man. Listen, when I was up on the bluff I noticed that downstream there are several trails – leastwise, they looked like trails – runnin' down the rock to the water. The hosses would swim for them – waal, it would be a chance."

From behind a rock a few yards away Marshal Matt Hollis aimed his Winchester at a gunflash and sent a .44 slug whistling in its direction.

"A chance to get yourself drowned," muttered Reno. "That'd be a helluva way to go, your belly full of water an' your lungs bustin'. Still, it would be a gamble. I figure the stakes are right. You game?"

"Yeah."

"Let's get back to the hosses, then. Hey, Hollis, get your boys to give us some coverin' fire."

"What you gonna do?" shouted the marshal.

"Don't you fret about that," retorted Reno. "Jest keep them fellas with their heads down for half a minute. Okay?"

"Guess so," Hollis growled reluctantly. His dislike of the bounty hunter had not lessened with his rescue of Victoria Grayson. Still, Reno was fighting on his side so he called out: "Hey, men, give those varmints a taste of lead."

A fusilade cracked across the ford. Echoes muttered to each other up and down the river. Billows

140

of smoke rolled lazily in the faint breeze, causing the eyes of the posse to water painfully.

"Right, boy," snapped Reno. With surprising agility for a man of his size he leapt up from behind the dead horse and ran doubled up towards the shelter of the rocky outcrop. Nathan, still limping slightly from his injured toe, floundered after him over the loose sandy soil.

A few seconds later the two men, their breath burning their throats, flung themselves to safety behind the outcrop where the posse's horses were hobbled.

Without a word Reno drew his guns and, threading his black silk kerchief through the trigger guards, tied them round his neck so that they hung down between his shoulders blades.

"Always keep your powder dry, my daddy often used to say," he muttered. "Can't recollect any other advice he gave me."

Nathan drew his Peacemaker and followed Reno's example, having first of all made sure that there was an empty chamber opposite the hammer so that he would not be shot in the back by accident.

"Let's go," Reno grunted, unhobbling his horse.

"See you on the other side, Mister Reno," replied Nathan, swinging into his saddle.

"Giddap!" shouted the bounty hunter and he ran the rowels of his spurs cruelly along the flanks of his skittering mount.

With dust spurting from their hooves, the two horses raced towards the ford. The posse turned and gaped in amazement as Reno and Nathan drummed past them and hit the water of the crossing with a dramatic splash. Seconds later the horses were swimming in the current while their masters had slipped from their saddles and, with only their heads above the surface, clung for dear life to their reins.

Bullets whipped the water close to Nathan but he paid no attention. Several times his head had gone under and he had sucked down mouthfuls of muddy water. A blind panic filled him. Was he drowning already? He coughed and spluttered, and when his head went under again into the wet, roaring darkness of the river lights exploded before his eyes.

Beside him his dark mare swam steadily, the current carrying her fast downstream. Soon both horses and their bedraggled riders were out of sight of the Crazy Steer ford. Nathan ventured to open his eyes and got the impression of steep walls of pinkish rock whirling past. He hastily closed them again.

After what seemed to be an eternity, but in reality was a few minutes, he felt his mount struggling for a foothold. A moment later he felt himself dragged from the clutch of the river and found himself on a narrow strip of silt. Releasing the reins, he vomited water and then looked up to see that Reno had made landfall a dozen yards farther down. The bounty hunter grinned sardonically at Nathan's white face.

"I'll be fine an' dandy in a minute," the young man gasped, and was sick again.

"Ol' Yellow ain't the sweetest in the world," consoled Reno while he carefully removed his spectacles from a pocket in his shirt and put them on. "I guess I should've told you to hold your breath when you went under Ain't you ever crossed a river afore?"

"Blamed lot of rivers there were for me to cross at Red Buttes," Nathan growled.

"Anyways, you were dead right about the trails comin' down the side," said Reno, pointing to a narrow ledge which ran at a steep angle up the river wall. It was obviously used by wild animals when thirst drove them in search of water. "I reckon we can lead our hosses up that without too much grief."

He untied his kerchief and checked his guns, then slid them into their wet holsters.

"C'mon, boy, we've got an appointment back at Crazy Steer." So saying he grasped the bridle of his horse and began to lead the reluctant beast up the slender path. Still spitting out the muddy taste of the Yellow River Nathan follov

CHAPTER ELEVEN

Chet Webb lay behind a slab of basalt. The sun gleamed on the octagonal barrel of his '73 Winchester rifle. Beyond it, over the clay-coloured water of the Crazy Steer ford, he could see an occasional puff of smoke as a member of the posse sent a bullet whining towards him and his comrades. For some time there had been a lull in the firing, each group realising that it was a waste of ammunition to fire volleys across the river when each had such good cover. Both parties were now waiting for a move from the other which would give their marksmanship a chance.

Several times Chet had considered breaking cover, running to the horses and galloping away down the trail to Jolita. But, he decided, it would be better to wait for nightfall. He had already lost a couple of men this morning and there was no point in taking an extra risk. He was convinced that a hex had fallen on him at the death of his brother Austin, and he was determined to be cautious. Come nightfall he and his remaining followers would melt away. And it was doubtful if the posse would dare to cross the ford in the dark.

His thoughts kept returning to his bad luck. To begin with the robbing of the Wheel of Fortune had seemed simple enough. It had been until that chance bullet had killed Austin. From then on things had gone wrong. There had been trouble with Hansen over the wretched schoolmarm, then this morning an unknown sniper had killed Sayce outright and Gower had vanished down the river after the same rifleman had shot his horse. Now he and his men were pinned down by a two-bit posse from Gila City . . . there surely was a hex on him all right!

His mind kept straying back to the dying face of his brother. He would have to write and tell his mother about it. The old lady was in Kansas, and he wanted her to know about it from him before she read it in some newspaper. Maybe, when the loot had been shared out in Jolita, he would quit the gang for a while and go and see her. He could not imagine much pleasure in the visit. Ma had always blamed him for leading Austin astray – as though he'd ever needed any leading!

"If you live by the gun you'll die by the gun sure as night must follow day," were the last words he remembered her saying to him.

Well, he'd lived pretty well by the gun so far. Far better than if he'd been some lousy cowhand or underpaid farm labourer.

He grinned slightly as he remembered a verse of poetry written by a hold-up man known as Black Bart. After each hold-up Bart would leave behind a few lines on a scrap of paper. These had been faithfully quoted on Wells Fargo reward posters. One of the poems read:

I've laboured long and hard for bread –
For honour and for riches –
But on my corns too much you've trod,
You fine-haired sons of bitches.

Black Bart sure knew what he was talking about. Chet couldn't have expressed his feelings better himself. He'd laboured long and hard on his old man's place and all that it had got him was calloused hands. Maybe if the Civil War hadn't lost them most of their land it would have been a different story, but that was history now and the lesson was clear. Life gave nothing but hard work to those who had lost the war. A man of spirit had to seize what he wanted by force. If he was strong enough – ruthless enough – he could carve out a reputation and a fortune at gunpoint. Yes sir, Black Bart understood life all right.

Still, he was worried by the hex. The gang had pulled off more dangerous jobs than this with no trouble. He'd have to be careful.

Something moved on the opposite bank. Chet squinted along the Winchester and fired. A cry of pain floated to him over the murmur of the ford. He grinned wolfishly.

Suddenly he heard Hansen give a shout: "Chet – behind you . . . !"

There was the crash of a Colt and Hansen screamed and rose drunkenly from behind his boulder. Several guns exploded on the other side of the ford. The bullets caught Hansen and sent him spinning grotesquely.

Chet rolled over and saw two men standing at the top of the slope which led down to the river. Both wore black, both held pistols and both were poised in the characteristic gunfighter's crouch. Smoke drifted from the muzzle of the taller man's gun. He was the one who had just shot Hansen from behind. Chet noticed that the sunlight glinted strangely on the tinted spectacles he wore.

"By Gawd, the hex!" Chet muttered to himself. There was something so sinister about the two black clad figures that to the gang leader they might almost have been angels of death.

Another of the Webb gang suddenly stood up and opened fire. The strangers replied, and while the air was filled with the blurred reports of the Colts, Chet jumped to his feet and dived in the direction of the horses. Bullets whistled about him from the opposite bank, but he ignored them. His one aim was to reach a horse, and it had to be his horse because of its bulging saddlebags.

The battle between the two gunfighters and the remainder of the gang continued, giving Chet the chance he needed to loosen the hobble and hurl himself into the saddle. Then with his own Peacemaker blazing he galloped up the trail. The strangers had taken cover as they shot it out with his companions, leaving the way clear for him. He sent a couple of .45 slugs in their direction as he passed, and then bending low, he spurred his quaking mount through a defile and out on to the open plain.

Behind him Reno moved out from behind the shoulder of rock where he had reloaded his guns and fired rapidly at a rifleman in a tartan shirt. To the bounty hunter the bright colours were the only indication of the enemy in his blurred vision. But it was enough. The rifle clattered to the rock as the outlaw rocked back with a smashed shoulder.

"I quit," he yelled at the top of his voice.

"It's okay, he's harmless," Nathan told Reno.

"That goes for me, too," said another man, standing up with his hands level with his shoulders.

147

"Now that Chet's run off with the coin there ain't no point in bein' shot to pieces."

Nathan covered the two men with his gun while Reno walked over and looked down at Hansen. On the other side of the river the posse was breaking cover and mounting their horses to cross over.

"Let's get after Webb," said Reno coming back to Nathan. "The marshal can look after these two."

A minute later Nathan and Reno were spurring their horses up the defile, following the hoofprints of the outlaw leader's mount.

"Can you see any sign of him?" shouted Reno as the two men galloped side by side. "My goddam sight ain't good today."

"I can't see him, but he must be somewhere ahead," Nathan yelled in reply.

"I want to get him before the others catch up," Reno went on, jerking his head back. Looking over his shoulder Nathan saw a small group of riders raising dust behind them. It was part of the posse led by Matt Hollis.

"Why not let them catch up, they might be useful if we get Chet Webb cornered."

"Chet Webb's got a thousand dollars on his head."

A look of understanding dawned in Nathan's eyes.

"You mean ..."

"Sure. We're gonna collect on Webb."

"So that is why you joined the posse."

"It seemed the smart thing to do."

"I thought we joined to help Miss Victoria."

"Waal, we did, didn't we."

148

A strange excitement filled Nathan. He was on a job at last with Reno, a real bounty job, and it was only now that he realised it. He laughed into the wind.

An hour passed. The posse was now riding close behind Nathan and Reno, and the youngster was afraid that his mare was starting to fail. The swimming of the Yellow River had probably tired her before they set out on the chase. Then, looking up into the shimmering distance, Nathan saw a faint cloud of dust hanging over the trail and blowing like whitish smoke over the irregular patches of grey-green sage.

"He's ahead all right, I can see his dust," Nathan told Reno at the top of his voice. "Guess his cayuse must be getting blown, too."

The bounty hunter said nothing but his lips compressed into a humourless smile.

"Keep goin', old gal," Nathan whispered to his horse. "Jest keep a-goin' a little longer an' then you can have a long rest an' the best oats money can buy."

As though she understood his words, the foam-flecked mare seemed to call on some hidden reserve of energy and her gait became more steady.

Now Nathan could discern Chet and his mount through the pall of dust. The outlaw's arm rose and fell as he belaboured his mount with a quirt.

"We'll soon have him, lads," cried a voice jubilantly.

Nathan looked to the right and saw that Hollis and his men were riding abreast of him. The sight of the fugitive had made them urge their mounts to greater efforts.

The marshal drew a Henry carbine from its saddle boot and held it ready for use once he drew within range. Inwardly Nathan cursed because he had left his Sharps on the west bank of the river. There had been no need to take it with him when he had swum his horse across, but if only he had it with him now he was sure that he would be able to drop Chet's horse even from such a distance.

Soon it became clear that the outlaw's steed was labouring. The hooves of the pursuers' mounts thudded rhythmically on the dusty trail, and every moment saw the narrowing of the gap between them and the fugitive. At last Hollis raised the Henry and fired a wild shot over his horse's head. Such a shot, fired from a galloping horse, had little chance of finding its mark, but the report had the effect of making Chet turn and look over his shoulder. Through the curtain of dust that hung behind him he saw a line of hard-riding men. It was obvious that soon they would overtake him. He began to fumble with his saddlebags.

A minute later one of the posse gave a whoop of astonishment.

"Look at what he's a-doin'," he cried.

Ahead of them Chet Webb was throwing handfuls of silver dollars in the air. Soon the riders were riding over the scattered coins which gleamed and glinted in the hot afternoon sun.

One of the men reined up and swung down. Another followed him. Frantically they began scooping up the money. When Chet threw down his second saddlebag, so that it burst like some, silver bomb, the marshal and the remainder of the posse halted and threw themselves on to the coin-littered trail.

"Six thousand dollars!" cried one man. "He's just thrown away six thousand dollars!" Not only was there coin scattered everywhere but paper bills fluttered in the light breeze like falling leaves. Some of the men began pursuing them with the same intensity as butterfly collectors. Only Nathan and Hannibal Reno continued the chase.

Suddenly Chet's horse seemed to sway, it missed its footing and then crashed down completely exhausted. The outlaw was out of the high Californian saddle and free of the stirrups almost before the poor beast had hit the ground. He stood waiting with his Colt in his hand.

"Split up," Reno shouted to Nathan. "Go right, I'll head left."

Nathan obeyed, and when he was still several hundred feet from the waiting gunman, he slid to the ground from his reeling mare. If he was going to use his gun accurately he would have to advance on foot. On the other side of the trail Reno followed his example. Now the three men formed a triangle, a triangle which continued to shrink as the bounty hunters closed in from different directions.

"I'll give you a chance to throw down your gun," Reno shouted. "You ain't got a hope against the two of us."

"Don't be too sure, mister," Chet yelled and he started to back along the trail. Suddenly Reno began to run towards him. It seemed a foolhardy thing to do but Nathan knew that it was because at such a distance the ailing eyes qf the tall man could not make out their target properly. Nathan likewise began to run. Chet calmly raised his gun and fired a shot in the direction of Reno. The range was still too

151

much for revolver shooting, but Nathan fired so as to distract the outlaw. He half turned and fired back at him. The bullet snipped leaves off a nearby sagebush.

Reno continued to race forward. Again Chet fired. Nathan dropped to one knee, and steadying his right wrist on his left forearm took careful aim.

Suddenly Reno saw his quarry come into focus as he neared him. This was the moment he had been waiting for. His gun swung up and he began to blaze away. At the same time Nathan opened fire again.

Chet Webb seemed to sway under the impact of the bullets. He fired once more at Reno, then the gun dropped from his limp hand. Turning, he began to stagger up the trail, rolling from side to side like a drunken man. Nathan lowered his gun and watched the swaying figure with grim fascination. Reno fired once more after taking cool aim. Chet's legs buckled under him. He collapsed and lay on his back, staring at the brazen sky above. As Nathan and Reno approached they saw his shirt was stained with the blood from several wounds. His eyes were glazing.

Carefully Reno knelt down beside him.

"Anythin' you want to say afore you go, Chet," he asked almost tenderly. To Nathan it seemed hardly possible that this was the same man who had taken such careful aim at his victim after he had dropped his gun.

With an effort Chet Webb turned his head so he could see Reno bending over him, and the figure of Nathan posed in the background.

"You fine-haired sons of bitches," he gasped and died.

* * *

The world beyond the open doorway was bright, too bright. The noon sun gave the landscape a quivering unreality in which even the brightest colours seemed washed out in the intensity of the light. Most citizens of Gila City had fled indoors to escape the painful brilliance and the waves of heat which seemed to tremble over the town like the air above a stove. They lay or lounged in sweaty discomfort, waiting for the cool which they knew would come and ease them at sundown. Many declared it was the hottest summer they'd known – and the driest drought.

In contrast to the heat outside, the interior of the Wheel of Fortune was darkly cool. Shutters were down to kill the glare and only the door remained open. In the background was the monotonous sound of a saw as a carpenter worked on repairing the damage done when the Webb gang blasted Fortune's safebox.

Now Fortune, rested after her hard riding with the posse, sat at a small table in the corner of the main room. Casually she lit one of her long, slim cheroots and blew a blue cloud of fragrant smoke towards Nathan Knight who sat opposite her, a tall glass of beer in his hand.

"So this will be your last day in Gila," Fortune was saying. "You intend to leave with your friend Reno."

Nathan nodded.

"I am sorry you are going, Nathan," said Fortune slowly. "You fitted in here at the Wheel.

But it is more than that. I know enough of the world now to realise that there are times when a woman should speak plain. To hide feelings – to play games with words, that is all right for young girls or prissy schoolmarms, but a real woman should never be afraid to say what she thinks. So, Nathan, I am asking you to stay."

"Aw, I guess you'll find someone easy enough to take my place here at the Wheel," Nathan said reassuringly. "There's plenty of tough *hombres* who'd jump at the job."

"Nathan, I can't make up my mind at times whether you are just natural-born stupid, or if you play act at being stupid. Listen, I wasn't talking about the job at the Wheel. I don't give a damn really about who carries a gun here at the moment, what I am saying is that I don't want you to leave Gila for... for... other reasons. Do I have to spell it out? For some reason I cannot understand I have grown very fond of you since you have been here. I know you like me, except you're also scared of me 'cause you ain't used to women ... and, well, I thought maybe you and I, Nathan .. ."

Nathan put his hand across the table and clumsily took hers. "I know what you mean," he said. "Believe me, I know 'cause you've been kinda on my mind too. Only, I guess I ain't right for you ... not yet, anyway. You're a rich woman, you've made a big success of all this..." He gestured vaguely round the Wheel of Fortune. "You're also a lady. You know how to act right. But I'm still a hick really. I've been lucky with my gun just now, but deep down I know that I ain't anythin' much.

154

Not yet anyways. That's why I have to go with Reno."

Although she had been speaking seriously, there was a hint of amusement in Fortune's cool eyes as she looked at the young man before her. He looked so much better now that he'd had that terrible shock of hair trimmed, she thought. And there was much more confidence in his features since that night when he had first walked into the Wheel of Fortune.

When Nathan looked down at his beer, not knowing what else to say, Fortune spoke. "Are you trying to let me down gentle, Nathan?"

He shook his head.

"If you want to make something of yourself you can do it here in Gila. I could stake you in some sort of business, or maybe we could work out something about a partnership in the Wheel."

"No. I must do it alone – or, at least, with Reno. Ever since I've met him I've felt my ... my ... what's the goddamn word?"

"Destiny?"

"Yeah, destiny. I've felt that my destiny was linked up with that guy somehow. I find it's hard to tell 'cause I guess I don't rightly understand it."

"Maybe I do," mused Fortune softly. "I've seen a man I loved ride off before – because of his destiny."

"Was he ..."

"Was he my lover?"

Nathan nodded.

"No, he was my brother. He went his way, I had to go mine. I started gambling ... and here I am."

"What about him?"

Fortune shrugged.

"He's around. Somewhere." She caught the eye of the barkeeper lounging behind the long counter. "Hey, Charlie. Better bring us over a bottle of Old Vermont. This conversation is in need of a lift."

"Here's to your journey," she said a moment later, lifting her glass. "Where are you heading?"

"I'm not sure," said Nathan, relieved that the conversation was getting more normal. "Reno has something on. He's all-fired about some letter he got just afore we went after Chet Webb and his lot. Guess I'll know soon enough."

"There is something sick about that man," said Fortune suddenly. "I wish to God you were not going with him. Go and follow your star if you must, but not with him."

"I know you don't like bounty hunters," Nathan muttered, "But he ain't that bad. He's a real man ..."

"Do real men live off blood money?"

"Look, the guys that Reno goes after ain't ordinary folk. They've all done something pretty mean, they've all spilled blood, otherwise there wouldn't be a price on their heads. The country is better off without them."

"Sure, sure, I know. You can make the same argument for the hangman." The blood drained from Nathan's face.

"I'm sorry. I said it because I care about you I suppose. I'm scared something in Reno will rub off on you. I'm older than you. I've seen these things happen. He's so ruthless. I feel that he just lives to kill. Oh yes, I know you can say that he helped save Victoria Grayson when he didn't need to so he can't be all that ruthless, but most of the time I was with the posse I got the feeling that he was waiting for the moment he would get his gun out and go for the kill. I know a killer nature when I meet it."

"It ain't that simple. I guess he can be ruthless. Fact is, when he put the last bullet into Chet Webb I felt bad. Chet was wounded serious, probably dyin', an' he'd lost his gun, an' Mister Reno takes slow aim an' lets him have the last shot in the back. That sure was a cold thing to do. But then, when Chet was layin' takin' his final breath, Mister Reno bends over him sorta tender and speaks real kindly to him. That wasn't ruthless."

"Maybe you've got it the wrong way round. Maybe that last shot was the kindness. Chet Webb was badly hurt. Even if he had lived all he could have expected was the gallows – or a lynching. But after that... well, I've heard tell that some hunters really love the animals they kill."

For a while the two sat in silence, each busy with their own thoughts. At last Nathan finished off his drink.

"Guess I'd better be goin'," he said. "I'd like you to know that I've been mighty proud to have met you. I hope I see you again some day ..."

"I'll always be glad if you come my way again," Fortune replied. "I have a hunch that our trails will cross. Be lucky."

Nathan pushed back his chair and his high-heeled boots clattered on the board floor as he marched across the room and out into the dazzling sunlight.

"By God," he murmured. "That Fortune is some woman." He was suddenly filled with anger at himself. If only he'd had some experience with women he'd have known what to have said. He'd spoken like a fool, when all the time there was so much that he'd wanted to say to her, only he just did not have the words.

He strode along the boardwalk in the direction of the town corral. Now a hot gust of desire was mingled with his anger. For a moment he paused. There was a choking feeling in his throat. In his imagination he saw the perfect features of Fortune Sarrat again with the usual, slightly mocking light in her eyes. He almost turned on his heel to go back to the gambling saloon.

"Goddamn it," he muttered, bewildered by his own hot emotions. Then, pulling himself together with an effort, he continued on.

Ahead he saw Marshal Matt Hollis leaning against a clapboard wall, passing the time with some loungers.

"On your way, Nathan?" he asked.

Nathan nodded. "That's right, Marshal."

"Good luck then, son. Not that I reckon you'll need much. When I put you in my lock-up when you first hit town I didn't figure I was jailin' such a wildcat."

He shook Nathan by the hand.

"I rather wish you was goin' on your own. There's somethin' about that Reno ... Anyways, *hasta la vista*"

"Hasta la vista."

When Nathan reached the Gila City Square-Deal Corral, he found Hannibal Reno sitting alone on the top rail of the high compound. At a nearby hitching post his black horse was saddled and ready for the trail.

"Sorry if I've kept you waitin'," said Nathan, hurriedly placing his saddle on his mare. "Time went kinda fast."

Reno smiled slightly. "At your age fond farewells take a mite of gettin' through."

Five minutes later the two men, dressed in their dark range-riding clothes and their worldly possessions in neat rolls behind their saddles, trotted their mounts through the wooden gateway of the corral and headed out of Gila City.

Just as they were passing the schoolhouse Victoria Grayson appeared at the door.

"Nathan, Mister Reno," she called. The two halted and politely removed their black, wide-brimmed hats.

"Before you go, I want you to know that you have my sincere thanks," she said in a low voice.

"That's all right, ma'am," said Reno. "Only happy to be of service. Everythin' worked out okay in the end."

"Yes, I understand you are claiming the reward for Chet Webb..."

Reno nodded but said nothing. There was a slight, ironical smile on his lips, but, because of his tinted spectacles, Nathan could not see what he was thinking.

Victoria came closer to Nathan, raising her hand and holding the mare's bridle.

"I truly wish you were staying here," she said. "I had thought that... that you and I... well, never mind. Perhaps some day you will come back to Gila City. But while you are gone, try and remember that life is not all violence ... and ... and death. There can also be happiness ... and love ... and a good life.

159

Just remember that. And please take this to read."

She held up a small booklet. Nathan took it and looked at the cover. It was entitled: "The Evils of Gambling."

"Thank you," said Nathan, pocketing the tract. "Guess I can hardly wait to read it."

"You're laughing at me," smiled Victoria. "I guess I just can't help trying to reform you. Now, you must go. Do not forget me, and I'll remember you in my prayers."

She turned hurriedly and re-entered the school house. The faces of the children, which had been pressed against the windows, vanished as if by magic.

"Love sure is a funny proposition," remarked Reno, "especially when you're young. But in the end it don't amount to much. It saps your freedom. An' I should know."

Nathan nodded.

"Yeah," he said. "I guess it could. Where are we headin', Mister Reno?"

"A little place called Esmerelda," replied the bounty hunter. "We've got some business there with a bank."

"Let's hit the trail then," Nathan cried, and as he touched his mare's flank gently with his spurs he felt as though a weight was rolling from him.

Reno's fine black mount leapt forward at the same moment and both riders galloped on to the trail which led north across the vast, sun drenched plain. Soon all that remained of their presence was a drifting haze of dust.

CHAPTER TWELVE

Jake Kelly shivered in the cold night wind and drew his sheepskin jacket closer about his broad shoulders. He had just ridden out of a belt of fragrant pines and now he halted his horse so that he could gaze down on the grassy slope which fell away at a steep angle until it was lost in the deep shadow of the mountain. Part of the slope was illuminated with startling brilliance by a moon of frozen silver. To anyone with an artistic sense the scene would have been breathtaking with its wild beauty. The pines appeared like finely detailed silhouettes against the snow-covered peak of the mountain, the sky was alive with flying scuds of cloud which appeared almost like a stampede of celestial mustangs, their outlines drawn in silver against the deep velvet of the night sky. Not even Jake Kelly's best friend – supposing that he had one – would have accused him of being artistic, yet even this shaggy, black-bearded wanderer felt a sense of awe as he looked down into the mystery of shadows below him.

"Sure is pretty," he remarked to his mount. "Yep siree, that sure is a picture." It was the only time in his usually violent life that Jake was moved by nature, and as he continued down the slope he felt an unfamiliar elation in his breast. He was cold and hungry, and he had travelled far over a rough trail, but now he did not mind. And suddenly he realised that the elation he felt was a sense of peace. It was heightened by a tiny spark of light below which seemed to wink at him like some far but friendly beacon.

Unfamiliar thoughts began to filter through his. head. If he was honest he must admit that lately he had been getting tired of his roving life, always on the move, never knowing where he would lay his head.

"Reckon a fella might do worse than get himself a parcel of land on a mountain an' raise hisself some cows an' steers," he murmured to himself. "With a good cabin a fella could live pretty well, an' right out of the way of strangers."

As his mount carefully picked its way down the slope the distant light began to assume a square shape, and after a while it became clear that it was a lighted window. Beneath his black whiskers Jake grinned a broken-toothed grin. Coming to this shack on the mountain was the nearest he had ever felt to coming home.

When he was only a hundred feet away he dismounted, and having tethered his horse to a piece of broken fencing, approached the shack on foot. In his hand he held a long-barrelled Navy Colt. Jake Kelly had been on the road too long to take chances. Moving silently as a shadow, he reached the wall and sidled along it until he was able to peer round the edge of the window. He saw a young, graceful woman seated at a table lit by, the soft yellow glow of a tall-chimneyed kerosene lamp. She was sewing. Beyond her Jake could make out some cooking pots steaming on an iron stove.

Gently Jake tapped the window. The girl started, got up and reached for an old Volcanic rifle

162

that was mounted on a couple of wall pegs.

"It's okay, Belle," he called. "It's me, Jake."

Immediately Belle ran to the door, threw it open and as Jake entered the warm room she flung her arms round him.

"Oh, Jake," she cried. "You've arrived just as you said you would. I was so sure you'd be on time that I've got supper cookin'."

"Sure smells dandy," said Jake, throwing off his sheepskin and settling in a chair by the warm stove. "Ah, this is good. It's durned cold outside. Let me warm up a mite an' then I'll go out an' see to Pepper. An' tell me, how's it been for my woman?"

"Lonely," said Belle with a sigh. "The nights have been long, Jake."

"Yeah,' he muttered gruffly. "Yeah. Belle, I was kinda figurin' tonight that it might not be such a bad notion to settle down soon, maybe get a parcel of land an' build a cabin. Some place where I'm not known. Then you an' I... waal, maybe things could work out like we usta talk about."

Belle looked at him with a strange expression in the soft light.

"Are you gettin' old, Jake," she asked with a slight laugh.

"Maybe just a little tired," he answered. "I been on the road a while now. I guess we wouldn't be troubled for money... it's safe isn't it?"

"Every dime," she replied. "It's under the floor, just where you buried it."

"Good," he said. "It'd be a fine stake to start on."

"What about Esmerelda. Are you still . . ."

163

"Sure, Belle," he laughed. "That would be too good to pass up. But after that . . ."

"You seem to be a changed man, Jake."

"Yeah, well... I guess I've been findin' the nights pretty long, too. There comes a time when a fella gets plumb weary of sleepin' on the trailside ... an' wonderin' where the next shot is gonna come from."

"You ain't losin' your nerve, are you, Jake?" Belle asked anxiously.

He roared with laughter.

"Jake Kelly lose his nerve," he cried, slapping his thigh so hard with his huge hand that it sounded like a pistol shot. "You must be kiddin'. Here, take a look at that. That don't say I'm losin' my nerve. They've upped the ante. Why it's the highest reward in the territory now."

From an inside pocket he took a folded piece of paper and flung it on the table. Belle picked it up and smoothed it out. Under the black heading of "WANTED – $3,000 REWARD" a picture of Jake gazed ferociously up at her.

"How's about that for a likeness?" he grinned.

She looked at it critically, her head on one side.

"They've got it better than they used to, when it was only a few hundred dollars."

"Yeah, I'm 'dead or alive' class now with a vengeance. The most wanted man in the territory. Ain't that a laugh, Belle. You could turn me in, Belle, an' make yourself a fortune."

She smiled.

"You're worth more alive to me than dead, Jake. Now, see to Pepper an' I'll serve up the meal. I got a bottle of Red Eye stashed away for afterwards."

"That's my Belle. I ain't had a drop since I held up a saloon at Hopkins' Crossin'"

"You held up a saloon?"

"Sure. An' I nearly bust laughin'. I jest went up to the bar, turned round an' said to the customers: 'Gen'lemen, I'm Jake Kelly an' I'd 'preciate if you'd shell out without unpleasantness.' You should have seen 'em. They started tossin' coin an' gold watches into my hat faster'n a lizard can blink. I didn't even have to pull out my iron. They knew it was me sure 'nough 'cause there was a big poster like that one tacked up on the wall. Then I had me a swallow of rye, bid them good-day an' hit the trail."

Belle laughed.

"You just don't care, do you. There might have been anyone in that bar, maybe some fast gun who would have given anythin' to take a shot at you."

"Not in Hopkins' Crossin'," he laughed. "You ain't never seen such a dead hole. Top guns like the lively towns. Hopkins ain't got no style for anyone. I felt almost ashamed to take the pickin's, but I was runnin' short of money, an' besides I felt like a drink."

The burly hold-up man climbed to his feet and lumbered through the door to look after his horse. Belle busied herself over her stove, a slight frown on her face.

Much later Jake Kelly lay back on the bed, an empty whisky bottle on the floor beside him and a beatific smile on his flushed face. At regular intervals a deep snore shattered the silence of the shack.

Belle looked at him intently for a minute, then carefully opened the door and walked into the night. Immediately a figure materialised out of the darkness.

"Belle, darling, is everything all right?"

She could just make out the young man's white features in the light of the sinking moon.

"Yes, Jack. Just as he had planned. He reckons on doin' the Esmerelda job tomorrow afternoon. So go an' give the word to Mister Myers."

"Yes, darling ..."

"Oh, Jack. Soon he'll be out of the way an' we'll be free to be together."

His arms were tightly round her now and he held her hard.

"An' we'll be able to dig up that loot," he murmured. "It'll all be ours. How much do you reckon ..."

"I must go back, dearest. Sometimes he wakes at the slightest sound. Get on your way to Esmerelda."

"The next time we meet we'll be free to be together, just as you said," he murmured in her ear. "There'll be no more fear of him turnin' up unexpectedly. An' with that loot I reckon I'll be able to buy a pretty nice little ranch ... uh, for you and me, of course."

"Of course," agreed Belle. "Now go, darling. Lord bless you."

"I'll be back when it's all over," he replied. And he vanished into the shadows whence he came.

* * *

A song growled from the throat of Jake Kelly as he rode down the trail which led along the valley floor in the direction of the small mining town of Esmerelda. The morning was hot and he rode with his sheepskin and his shirt open, exposing a tangle of black hair which covered his heavy chest. Life for

Jake was good. Despite the whisky he still- carried the mood which had settled upon him the night before. It had been good to be with Belle again, good to drink his fill of Red Eye without the fear of losing his safety, and it had been good to think about the future.

He was also satisfied he had done what he had set out to do. In his way, thanks mainly to the men he had gunned down and the publicity of wanted posters, he was a well-known character. Even famous. And he had made a fair pile while he had been on the road. He knew that if he settled down in some far place where the posters had not reached, he would probably miss the excitement of waiting for a stage coach to lurch round a bend to brake to a dusty halt before his gun, or the fun of watching the mouths of clerks drop open when he raced into some bank with the time-honoured words, "This is a raid and I'm a desperate man."

But there would be compensations. Maybe Belle and he might even raise some kids. Yes siree, now was the time to stop, especially as he began to get an inkling of his age. Often his left leg was stiff through rheumatism which had come as a result of sleeping rough and going for days in wet clothing when he was on the run from some posse or band of vigilantes.

So now he was riding to his last job. Well, it would be a good one, something for him to be remembered by. He knew that there would be a goodly amount of gold dust in the Esmerelda Miners' and Graziers' Deposit and Loan Bank. Earlier on careful investigation had elicited the knowledge that a cargo of dust left the bank by a specially guarded coach at the end of each month. During the month the amount would build up in the bank's special safe (the key of which the manager, Dudley Myers, wore round his neck on a steel chain). Tomorrow the bullion coach would arrive, but it would be too late. Today Jake planned to walk out of the Miners' and Graziers' with a month's accumulation of gold which had been won from the sluice boxes in the surrounding hills.

Esmerelda seemed deserted as he cantered down the main (and only) street. Few people lived there, the local population being scattered about the surrounding country where they worked their claims or tended their stock. Thus, apart from half a dozen shacks, Esmerelda consisted of a stage office, a blacksmith's, two saloons – the Lucky Miner and the Silver Dollar saloon – a general store, a combined stable and grain merchant's, a jail which had become the home for the town drunk, a gunsmith's and, at the end of the street, the false-fronted edifice which bore the ornate legend of the deposit and loan bank.

It was here that Jake reined up and tied his horse to a hitching rail, using a crafty knot which could be released by a quick tug. It was ideal for those who, for reasons of business, depended on being able to make a quick getaway. He loosened the long-barrelled gun in his holster, checked that a neatly folded linen bag was in the pocket of his sheepskin, and strode into the bank.

A young clerk looked up over the counter.

"Mister Myers?" said Jake politely.

The clerk nodded to a door on which the word "Manager" was inscribed in letters of gold leaf.

"Obliged," muttered Jake to the clerk, and he walked into the manager's office without the formality of knocking, Dudley Myers was a bald, corpulent little man who wore a tight black suit and had a pince-nez balanced on the button of his nose. He looked up from his desk with a slight frown.

"Can I be of some help to you, sir?" he inquired. He rather regretted having to use the word "sir" to such a character, but one could never tell with these miners. The roughest looking louts sometimes had a fortune in gold dust in wash leather bags in the pockets of their tattered Levis.

"You surely can be of help, mister," replied Jake Kelly with a grim smile. "Fact is you're gonna help me more than you know."

. A brief look of recognition seemed to pass over Myer's features.

"Haven't I ..."

"Maybe, mister, if you read reward posters." Casually Jake drew his Colt, and cocking back the hammer, pointed it at the generous curve of the bank manager's belly.

"I'm Jake Kelly," he said. "I've come to rob your bank. Now, if you kinda co-operate with me you'll be left with a good story to tell, but if you get any sassy ideas you'll be left with an extra navel. I've killed many men an' my stomach don't turn none at the sight of blood."

"I... I know all about you," stuttered Myers. "But you'll have difficulty in robbing this bank. Yes, sir, it has one of the finest safes that money could buy."

169

"I know," Jake said. "It's almost as big as a small room an' a whole barrel of blastin' powder wouldn't touch it."

"That's right," said Myers with a slight touch of pride. "There's a lot of gold mined round here and we've gone to a lot of trouble to guard it."

"That's mighty wise of you," said Jake. "Say, is that a box of cigars on your desk. Mind if I have one. I've gotta sorta weakness for a good cigar."

"I'm hardly in the position to refuse you," said Myers, pushing the box across.

Jake took a cigar, rolled it by his ear with his left hand and pronounced it satisfactory,

"Now, back to the problem of the safe," he said as he lit up. "Every safe has gotta have a key, an' I figure that you'll be obligin' me with it …"

"No," Myers declared. "It is always kept in a secret place. It would be unethical for me to divulge its whereabouts. You may have the – uh – drop on me, but I am a bank manager and it is my duty to protect my bank's property."

Jake inspected the glowing end of his cigar thoughtfully.

"Did you ever hear what the Webb gang did to a bank manager once," he said conversationally. "Seems like they wanted to get a safe combination out of a fella so to help him remember they poured the kerosene out of a lamp over his feet an' then set his boots on fire. Now, I kinda figure that was cruel. I mean, just imagine a fella dancin' round his office with his feet on fire. He'd probably never walk right again."

There was a silence.

Myers looked pale and uncomfortable.

"You wouldn't..."

Unexpectedly Jake chuckled in his black beard.

"No, mister, I ain't gonna be that mean to you. You see, I know where that key is. It's on a steel chain round your neck. Now, take it off and go to the safe an' open it. An' on the way tell your clerk not to raise any fuss or the lead will start to fly something dangerous."

"All right, Kelly, I guess you win," murmured Myers. He got up and went to the office door. Jake walked close behind him, the muzzle of his Navy Colt pressed hard into the tubby bank manager's spine.

"Please keep calm, Bob," Myers said hastily to his clerk as the strangely assorted pair stepped into the main office. "This is a hold-up. This man has a gun in my back and there is nothing we can do." At the last piece of information Bob looked relieved. He had no wish to play the hero when the tall, savage-looking stranger seemed so entirely in command of the situation,

"Against the wall, fella," Jake ordered. "Keep your hands up high so I can see you ain't plannin' on playin' no tricks."

Bob obeyed. Myers led the way over to a large steel door set in the wall.

"Like you said, it sure seems a might pretty safe," said Jake. He stood in the middle of the floor while Myers fumbled for the key which, just as Jake had been informed, was at the end of a chain round his fat neck. With his left hand the robber drew out his linen bag, and his dark eyes flashed with the fore-

171

taste of the pleasure he would have in filling it with the precious mineral which had held such a fascination for him ever since he was a small boy.

The key clicked in the lock. With a slight groan the heavy door swung outwards. As he pulled it open Myers suddenly skipped to one side. Framed in the steel-lined opening stood the black-garbed figure of Hannibal Reno. Before the startled Kelly could fire, the bounty-hunter's ivory-butted Colt spat orange flame and a .45 slug tore into the burly body of the robber. He staggered back under the impact, but gamely raised his gun to fire at Reno. His bullet went wild, striking the steel door and ricocheting through a window with a musical tinkle of shattered glass.

Reno fired again, and so did Nathan who had appeared, gun in hand, at the main door of the bank. Both bullets struck Jake, whirling him grotesquely across the floor until he struck the counter and collapsed. With their smoking pistols covering him, Reno and Nathan advanced until they both stood over him. But it was obvious that he was no longer a danger. His breath came in sobbing gasps and his face was a white mask of pain.

"I was ... sure fooled ... this time," he murmured. "You're Reno ... ain't you?"

"The same," said the bounty hunter, bolstering his Colt.

"Should have known ... that reward..." A trickle of blood ran from his lips into his black beard.

"Bob, run for the doc," Nathan shouted to the clerk, who looked as though he was about to pass out himself.

"We're gettin' you a doc," Reno said softly.

"I ... figure this is the ... end of the road,"

gasped the wounded man. "It weren't such a bad road."

"You got the highest price on you in the territory," Reno said,

Jake nodded,

"Yeah, I got big enough to interest you... didn't I, Reno?"

Reno nodded.

A red stain began to creep from under the bank robber's body.

"Reno ... will you ... do somethin' for me?"

"Say on."

"In my pocket... a gold watch. Didn't steal it... usta belong to my pappy ... give it to Belle ... my woman ... lives in a cabin up on Ole Whitetop . . . she'll understand."

"I'll surely do that," Reno said.

Suddenly Nathan felt strange. In the last few weeks he had got used to violent death, but now, suddenly, there were tears running down his cheeks. Abruptly he turned and ran out of the bank. Here he leaned against the clapboard wall and tried to control himself.

"Goddamn it," he muttered to himself, "He was only a murderin' skunk."

He drew his hands across his eyes savagely. When he looked up he saw a frock-coated man carrying a doctor's bag shoulder his way through the small crowd which had been attracted by the sound of the gunfire.

Several minutes later he came out of the bank in the company of Reno and Myers.

"There was nothing I could do for him," he said.

"He sure died game," Reno muttered. "Where do I find this Belle, this woman he spoke of. He wants her to have his watch."

"I shouldn't bother," said Myers. "It was Belle who gave me the tip-off about this raid some weeks ago. That was why I wrote to you, Mister Reno. And, I must say, you and you're partner have done a fine job. Obviously the bank will recompense you, and I understand there is a substantial reward for Kelly as well."

"But why did she tip you off?" asked Reno.

"She wanted him out of the way. She lived in terror of him because she'd fallen for some other fellow. It was he that came down early this morning to say Kelly was coming as he'd planned."

"Like I've said before, love sure is a funny proposition," Reno remarked to Nathan. "Still, Belle is gonna get his watch whether she wants it or not. An' if her fancy fella's about he'll get somethin' as well, somethin' he won't forget for a mite of time."

"Amen to that," said Nathan.

But, when the pair arrived at the shack on the slope of Old Whitetop the following day, there was no sign of Belle and her Jack. The only indication of them that remained was a large, hastily dug hole in the centre of the floor.

CHAPTER THIRTEEN

The eerie wail of the speeding locomotive split the night. In the moonlight the wraith of steam ribboning from the whistle appeared like a ghostly pennant. The wheels of the swaying train clacked on the lines of the trestle bridge and a shower of crimson sparks vomited from the wide funnel-shaped smokestack.

"That was Number 3 bridge, weren't it?" asked the handcuffed man in the brake-van. The brakeman nodded.

"Sure is, Silver," he replied, his eyes down on the fan of cards in his hand.

"That means we'll be in Stone Tree in a couple of hours?"

"That's about the size of it, Silver."

The man called Silver sighed.

"Then I'll need a bit of luck to get my money back before I'm thrown in the hoosegow," he grinned. "Come on, Reno, ante up."

In the dim light of a lantern Reno, Nathan, their captive and the brakeman sat round a packing case playing poker. It was some months after Jake Kelly had died on the floor of the Esmerelda Miners' and Graziers' Deposit and Loan Bank. Winter had come and Nathan and Reno had followed many trails fruitlessly. Their luck had changed when they got on the track of Billy Silver, a young man noted for his skill as a train robber. They ran him to earth in a hotel room in a small railway town by the name of Grand Falls. He had been lying on his bed, his hands beneath his head staring at the stained ceiling, when the two men, looking rather alike in their dark clothes, burst in with their guns drawn.

"Don't bother to shoot me," Silver had said calmly. "I've heard about you two guys, an' I know when the drop is on me."

"Now that's what I call a mighty sensible attitude, son," remarked Reno, taking out a pair of handcuffs. "It makes no difference to the reward whether I bring you in alive or dead."

Now Billy Silver and his captors were on their way to Stone Tree where the young railway robber was to stand trial. He accepted his capture philosophically and was soon on good terms with both Nathan and Reno. To while away .the time in the swaying brake-van he had suggested a hand of poker. Soon it was evident that his luck was out.

"Still, you may as well have it," he laughed good naturedly. "It's really railroad money."

The brakeman snorted.

"It's the last railroad money you'll gamble for a while," he grunted. "I reckon Central Pacific'll be mighty glad to hand over the reward to Reno and Knight for gettin' you out of the way."

"Waal, it was fun while it lasted," said Silver. "Reckon Leavenworth'll seem pretty tame ... C'mon, Reno, put up your stake."

Reno threw his cards down on the packing case top.

"Count me out," he said gruffly. "I don't feel like playin' no more."

Nathan looked sharply at his companion, but his large face conveyed no expression, and the young man was not able to see his eyes behind his tinted spectacles.

"That's a shame," Silver said. "I was hopin' for a bit of revenge .. .."

"Here, take your money," said Reno, fumbling for the pile of dollars before him. "We're makin' enough out of you as it is. You'll want it for a good lawyer."

"You won it fair an' square," began the prisoner.

Reno did not reply but leaned back against the wooden wall of the brake-van.

"Don't argue with Mister Reno," said Nathan. "He's bad medicine to argue with."

The remainder of the journey passed in silence apart from the sound of the wheels on the railroad tracks and the occasional banshee cry of the whistle.

When the train panted into Stone Tree the town marshal was waiting with a couple of deputies to take over the prisoner.

"S'long, fellas," said Silver as he climbed stiffly down. Reno remained lounging against the wall until he had been taken away.

The brakeman coughed, aware that something was going on that he could not quite understand.

"You'll have to get out now, boys," he said, "unless you wanna travel on to Utopia Junction."

"Nathan," said Reno. "Help me down."

"Sure, Mister Reno," he replied, the sickening truth of his comrade's plight dawning on him. He crossed the car and took Reno's arm.

"This way, Mister Reno ... there's a step here .. .."

When Reno was standing on the track beside the train Nathan looked up at the brakeman.

"Mister Reno's had a dizzy spell," he said. "Guess it was somethin' he ate."

"Sure, sure, if you say so," said the brakeman. He signalled with his lantern. The locomotive spat out gusts of steam and began to slide into the night. A minute later Reno and Nathan stood alone by the lines with the red tail light of the train vanishing into the darkness.

"Is it bad, Mister Reno?" Nathan asked.

"Yeah. When I was playin' poker I suddenly couldn't see the pasteboards no more. It's the first time my sight has gone completely."

"Can you see anythin' now?"

"No. It's just like I'm blind ... goddam it, I suppose I am blind."

"Don't fret too much," said Nathan. "I'll get us to a roomin' place, an' then I'll get a doctor."

"As you say. I guess I'm in your hands now, boy."

"In that case, will you quit callin' me 'boy.' "

"As you say, Nathan."

An hour later the tall, gangling doctor with the soft voice straightened up after peering intently into Reno's eyes.

"Waal, doc, shoot," Reno drawled. "Do I stay blind. Let's have it straight."

"I am not a specialist," said the doctor. "Since I've been in Stone Tree I've mainly treated fevers, bullet wounds, colic ... the usual afflictions that one finds here. But, when I was a student, I did put in extra study on the eyes. Perhaps in those days I did think I might become a specialist, but..." He shrugged. "Anyway, I am sure your sight will return. The eyes themselves are in no way damaged, and from what you tell me of the history of your complaint, I think that you may have intermittent pressure on the optic nerve."

"So what does that mean?" asked Nathan.

"It means that your friend's sight will be fair one day and bad another. It is indeed possible that this temporary blindness could come again. The fact that bright light does distress you, Mister ... Um, supports my theory."

"But what can I do, doc?"

"Nothing here in Stone Tree. I would suggest that you go East and consult a specialist. Perhaps an operation might remove the pressure on the nerve."

"You mean, have my head cut?"

"That's putting it crudely, but that's what I do mean."

Reno shuddered on his bed.

"I've had bullets dug out before now," he said. "Even watched it bein' done ... but I don't want no knife slicin' round my eyes."

"Well, that is up to you, of course," said the doctor, snapping his bag shut. "I would suggest meanwhile that you avoid strong light. If you have to travel, ride early in the morning or late afternoon."

"The sundown trail..." murmured Reno.

"I beg your pardon?"

"Nothin', doc."

"Will the attacks get worse?" asked Nathan. "Is there any way he'll know when they're comin' on?"

The doctor shook his head.

"When a nerve is involved the condition can change instantaneously ..."

"Come again?"

"At a moment's notice."

"That's dangerous in my profession," Reno said. . "What is your profession, may I ask?"

"Hoss-dealer," interjected Nathan swiftly. "You see, sometimes them hosses get mighty frisky an' you have to keep your eyes about you . . ."

"I see," the doctor said. "It isn't often one meets a horse-dealer who carries two guns ..."

"How much do I owe you, doc?" Reno asked.

"A couple of dollars. I'll send over some lotion which may help a little. Put it on when your eyes feel sore or strained. They have become very sensitive to light and this may help a little."

"One thing, doc," said Nathan as he showed the medical man to the door of the modest hotel, "keep it under your hat about my pal's little trouble. Okay?"

The doctor smiled slightly.

"Don't worry," he said. "I wouldn't want to get into trouble with Hannibal Reno. Good night."

Back in the room Nathan locked the door. "Remember what the doc told you," he said. "Come tomorrow you'll mebbe be able to see."

"Yeah," Reno murmured. "Mebbe."

"Anyways, I reckon it's lucky you let me come along with you. I said at the time I'd be your eyes."

"You're good enough to be on your own, now. I won't take it bad if you quit. It could be I'm finished."

"Don't talk loco, Mister Reno," Nathan

exclaimed. "We're pards, ain't we ... ain't we?"

"Sure," said Reno. "That's just what we are." As Nathan went to sleep a little while later there was a smile on his face.

The sound of Reno moving about the room woke him. Early morning light streamed through the window, and Nathan could see the tall bulk of the bounty hunter outlined against it.

How ... how are them eyes of yourn?" he asked.

"Fine," laughed Reno. "I can see better than I have for months. Maybe the trouble I had last night was the end of it."

"Say, that's mighty fine," cried Nathan. "We'll be on the trail again pronto. Who is the next on the list." Reno turned round.

"There is one guy I've always wanted to go after," he said. "He's got a big reward on him, but that – for once – ain't the only reason."

"Who is it?"

"A fella known as Lightnin' – Lightnin' Floyd."

"Floyd?"

"He operates east of the Sierra Madre, an' he's robbed more banks than you can shake a stick at. He's got a hatred for banks the same as the James boys have for railroads. But he's not only a robber, he's just about the best gunfighter in New Mex an' North Texas."

"Sure, I've heard tell of him," said Nathan. "He's a loner, ain't he?"

"If you're as good as Lightnin' Floyd you don't need a gang."

"An' you wanna bring him in?"

181

"He's the biggest fish for us to catch, Nathan. I reckon it'd be a mighty prideful thing to draw a bead on a fella like that."

The tall bounty hunter seated himself on his rumpled bed and lit a long black cigar.

"You know, Mister Reno, I just figured somethin' out about you," said Nathan.

"Say on."

"I always figured you were in this for the money. I figured you were a top gun an' you put it to use to make a pile on the right side of the law. But the way you talked about Lightnin' Floyd jest now made me realise you *like* manhuntin'. It's got to be some kinda sport with you."

Reno exhaled a blue cloud of cigar smoke.

"There ain't no sport with guys like Billy Silver, or even Jake Kelly," he said finally.

"Yeah, but there is with fellas like Chet Webb, or this Lightnin' Floyd – or the Dancer Brothers who I've heard tell were worthy of your gun."

"So, is it a crime to enjoy huntin'? What's with you, Nathan? You useta take your ol' Springfield an' go after animals round Red Buttes. You was always boastin' once how you shot an eagle on the wing. Waal, the game I've gone after is a mite more dangerous. It can shoot back. It's a question of me or the other guy – an' what makes it better is that I can understand the other guy. When the showdown comes I reckon I almost know what the other guy is feelin'..."

"But that doesn't stop you pullin' the trigger."

"Hell, no. It makes it all the better. Can't you understand ... haven't you felt it yourself?"

"No."

"Then what in the name of tarnation do you feel?"

"I – I don't know. But I don't *enjoy* it..."

"Are you sure? Are you kiddin' yourself you don't feel good deep down inside you when you see a fella in the sights of your gun an' know for sure that when you pull the trigger you're gonna drop him? Don't you feel *power?*"

For a moment Nathan said nothing. He was not used to such outbursts from the normally taciturn Reno.

"I guess Fortune was right about you," Nathan said finally, almost with reluctance.

"Ha, you've been listening to goddam woman talk," Reno cried. He drew furiously on his cigar. "I'll be damned. That female gambler put a seed in your mind an' it's jest startin' to flower now. An' all this time I figured you wanted to come along with me because you were like me, because you understood ..."

Both men were silent for a while, neither knowing what more to say.

"Mebbe we've been gettin' each other wrong, Mister Reno," Nathan said quietly at last. "But the last thing I want is to fall out with you. You've kinda given me somethin' I never had before. Anyways, I'll be happy to take the trail with you when you go after Lightnin'."

Reno said nothing for a while.

"No hard feelings, I hope, Mister Reno," Nathan said.

Reno laughed suddenly. "I need you too much to have any grudge. An' anyways, why the hell should I? You ain't insulted me. I guess you wanted to team up with me because you were a nothin' from nowhere – you wanted to become somethin' or somebody. Waal, I guess you have. You've got quite a reputation as a gunslinger. I guess I started on the bounty huntin' business for a different reason. Maybe it was because I wanted revenge."

"Revenge for what?"

"Revenge for somethin' that happened a long time ago. I thought I'd got revenge at the time, for I killed the fella who'd caused me the grief, but maybe killin' him was jest not enough, I had to keep on gettin' revenge."

"Was it over a woman?" Nathan asked, emboldened by Reno's unexpected talk about himself.

For a moment the bounty hunter inspected the ruby tip of his cigar.

"It don't matter what it was about now," he said at length. "It's an old story, an' I was mighty young at the time. Mebbe life wouldn't have turned out all that different if it hadn't happened. You can't tell. Let's forget the past."

He took out a sheath of handbills, wanted notices which he always carried. He passed one over to Nathan.

The young man looked at it and whistled.

"Ten thousand dollars," he exclaimed. "Five thousand for capture an' five thousand on conviction."

"Same as for Jesse James," said Reno. "That Lightnin' is worth goin' after. Reckon the banks've got together to put up a stake like that."

"They must want him bad," Nathan agreed. He studied the artist's impression of the wanted man on the creased paper. "It's a funny thing, but I've got a feelin' I've seen that fella someplace," he added thoughtfully.

"If you have, you'll be seein' him again," Reno said with a short laugh. "Now, come on, let's go an' collect the bounty on Silver an' then we can leave on the noon train. I got a funny feelin' Stone Tree ain't a lucky place."

A little later the two men left the hotel and began to walk across the town square, known locally as the Plaza. When they were in the centre Nathan saw three men walking purposefully towards them from the opposite side.

"Hey, Reno." called the one who seemed to be the leader. "I got somethin' for you ..."

Reno and Nathan paused and watched them approach.

When they were a dozen yards away the trio halted.

"You may not know me, Reno," the leader continued, " 'cause I guess it's sometimes hard to recognise a fella by the sound of his voice, an' by all accounts you can't see much behind them coloured glasses of yourn ..."

Nathan stiffened. He looked at Reno who was standing relaxed, his hands hanging loosely at his sides. "I don't quite follow you," Reno said.

"Rooms have thin walls at the Plaza Hotel," said the man with a grin. "The word has got round that you're blind, Reno. So you're no longer the gunman you was when you went after the Dancer Brothers – *my* brothers, Reno. I'm Tim Dancer."

Beside Nathan Reno moved his head round in a bewildered fashion. To any onlooker it would seem as though he could not see properly, that he was desperately trying to locate the direction from which

Tirn Dancer's voice came.

"This is a sweet moment for me, you bounty-huntin' son-of-a-bitch," he said. As he spoke his hand flashed down to the holster at his side. His two companions reached for their guns simultaneously.

But at the moment Dancer's hand began to move downwards Reno went into action. As if by magic his bone-handled Colt appeared in his hand and the first of a volley of .45 slugs whistled towards his enemies. Almost as fast, Nathan swung up his gun and joined in the rapid fire.

For several seconds the noise of the five revolvers blended in a single, prolonged crash of gunfire. Then Tim Dancer began to reel backwards, his gun continuing to explode uselessly, its bullets throwing up puffs of dust from the surface of the square. The man beside him gave a high-pitched squeal of agony, clasped his belly and toppled forward. Seeing his two companions fall the third man turned and began to run across the Plaza.

Nathan raised his smoking gun to eye level, rested his gun-hand on his left forearm and took careful aim.

"Give it to him," snapped Reno.

Nathan's trigger finger tightened. The bullet caught the fugitive in the leg, causing him to roll over and over before he came to rest by the wheel of a dray.

Reno surveyed the scene of battle through drifts of black powder smoke.

"You don't wanna believe everythin' you hear through the walls of a hotel room," he said to the world in general.

* * *

Summer had come again.

Nathan and Reno sat at the trailside while coffee simmered over a small brushwood fire. Nearby their hobbled mounts browsed contentedly.

"You know, it must be jest about a year since you followed Lorenz Seguro along the Red Buttes trail," said Nathan thoughtfully.

"That so?" muttered Reno. "Waal, boy, you've come a long way since then."

"Please, Mister Reno, don't keep callin' me..."

"This is how they write you up now," the bounty hunter interrupted, withdrawing a folded newspaper page from his waistcoat pocket. "Here, read it." He held it out.

"You read it to me," Nathan said. "You know I ain't that all-fired good at spellin' out words."

Reno adjusted his tinted spectacles, coughed and said: "It's headed BOUNTY HUNTERS BRING TERROR TO DESPERADOS, an' the story reads 'Thanks to the efforts of two men who are in the business of collecting rewards for the capture or otherwise of desperadoes wanted by the law, the State of Arizona has become an unhealthy place for those outcasts of society whose crimes warrant prices being put on their heads. One of the two has had a reputation for smart gunplay for many a season. He is Hannibal Reno who needs little introduction to the readers of this journal following the destruction of the infamous Webb gang. His comrade-at-arms, Nathan Knight, is a newcomer to the rough and ready world of freelance law enforcement, but already his skill with the 'hardware from Hartford' has gained him a reputation which many an experienced practitioner

187

at the art of shooting must envy.

"'In the past twelve months several hardened and dangerous criminals have paid the penalty for their crimes thanks to the skill and courage of these men. Their list includes, apart from the Webb Gang, Jake Kelly, Billy Silver, the rustler "Bloody Joe" Thomas and the notorious horse thief G. G. Berry.

"'When Hannibal Reno was interviewed by your reporter recently, he said: "It isn't the outlaws who worry me – my problem is trying to get the money out of the authorities after I have brought them in." It should be noted in passing that Reno and Knight more often bring in their quarry "dead" than "alive," which saves the State the cost of trials which can only end with the verdict of guilty no matter how eloquent the defence. Speculation is rife as to where Reno and Knight will strike next, but one thing is certain and that is the approach of this man-hunting pair is the signal for the hurried departure of thieves, thugs and bunko-steerers.'"

"What paper is that?" asked Nathan.

"The one that's printed at Gila City," Reno replied. "It's also got a little news item that may interest you."

"Yeah?"

"Yeah, it says the engagement is announced between Miss Victoria Grayson and the Reverend Hamilton P. Hogg."

"I sure hope they'll be very happy," Nathan said. "At least she won't have to refor

CHAPTER FOURTEEN

Ten miles east of Gila City there is a low but steep range of hills. As the trail from Gila approaches this natural barrier, it curves up from the plain to a V-shaped gap in the range which is known by the rather obvious name of Backsight Pass. It was here that Hannibal Reno and Nathan Knight waited one morning with the intention of ambushing the bank robber known as Lightning Floyd.

With a long brass Army telescope Nathan surveyed the trail east of Backsight Pass from a vantage point just above the gap. From this spot he could not only see the trail either side of the range, but he could command most of the pass itself, with his new hammerless Sharps-Borchardt target rifle for which he had traded in his buffalo gun. (Like many other expert shots, Nathan believed this to be the finest firearm the Sharps Rifle Company had ever produced before it suspended its operations in 1881.)

"Do you want to take a look through this spyglass?" Nathan asked Reno who was stretched out on hot rock beside him.

The bounty hunter shook his head.

"My damn eyes ain't much good today," he explained. "I guess I wouldn't make out a durned thing. But you keep watchin', he could come any time now."

"You sure seem to have a good idea of what he's plannin' to do."

Reno smiled slightly.

"I get information sent to me from round the country as you know. It costs but it's part of the expenses of the job. In the last few weeks I've picked up quite a lot about our pal Lightnin'. When he robbed the Samarra Bank the day afore yesterday I figured he'd pass this way."

"He might equally 'have headed back to his usual stampin' ground across the Sierra Madre ..."

"Accordin' to the telegraph I got from Samarra he stopped a bullet from one of the bank tellers."

"So...?"

"That makes me figure he'll head this way. We'll see soon enough."

Time passed. The heat intensified. Sweat soaked the shirts of the two men.

"I found out why Lightnin' has such a down on banks," Reno murmured conversationally. "Seems like there was a swindle down south an' a bank failed, wipin' out his family fortune. Seems they lost their ranch an' everythin'. 'Cause Floyd ain't his real name . ."

"There's a dust cloud," interjected Nathan. "It's a mighty long way off, but I guess there's a rider comin' up the trail."

"Could be Lightnin'," said Reno. "Sure hope so. It's blamed hot up here. I'll be glad to get it over. When he gets up the trail do you reckon you can pick off his cayuse. I want him alive. Remember half the reward depends on his *conviction*. The banks really want their money's worth."

"Reckon I can with this beauty," said Nathan, patting the long octagonal barrel of the gun. He raised the rear sight and squinted through it.

190

"I'll get the hoss the moment it reaches the top of the pass. Seems a damn shame to have to drop the poor crittur, but I guess there's no other way."

"It ain't your horse," Reno remarked. "As soon as it falls keep Lightnin' covered. I'll go on foot an' disarm him."

"Let's see that poster again," said Nathan. "I don't want to fire at the wrong guy."

Reno took out the crumbled handbill and once again Nathan looked at the confident features of the young robber.

"He ain't a bad lookin' guy," he said. "Looks like he could be a whole lot of fun."

"Providin' you ain't behind the counter of a bank," said Reno.

"Where was he wounded?" Nathan asked.

"The back. Shucks, there wouldn't be nobody crazy enough to draw a gun on him face on."

Nathan continued to watch the dust cloud through the circular eye of the telescope. Now he could make out the tiny image of the horse and rider.

"Be a while before he gets up to the pass," he commented.

He raised himself up slightly and looked in the opposite direction, across the plain towards Gila City.

"Hey, there's someone headin' this way from town," he exclaimed.

"That ain't unusual," Reno said. "Jest let's hope they don't get in the way. But don't fret about it none."

"It looks like a rider comin' up the trail to the pass." He raised the telescope to his eye. "It's a woman," he cried. "I can't see her face but she's got a ridin' skirt on."

"Don't worry about her," said Reno impatiently. "How about that fella comin' along the trail." Nathan swung round the telescope and refocused it.

"It looks like him," he said after a few moments. "I can just start to make out his face. He's got a little beard like the man in that picture."

Several minutes passed in silence while Nathan continued to follow the progress of the lone rider.

"Yeah," he said finally. "It's the same guy as on that 'wanted' poster. It's Lightnin' all right."

"Good," murmured Reno with satisfaction. He removed his tinted spectacles and polished them carefully. Nathan noticed that his eyes were inflamed.

"Have you put that lotion on your eyes today, Mister Reno?"

"It don't seem to do no good," Reno grunted. "Maybe when we've collected on Lightnin' I'll go East an' see what can be done. Wish to hell I could see better today – today of all days!"

"A pity it weren't sundown," said Nathan. "You always see better when the glare goes."

"Anyways, I'll get down to the pass," Reno said, preparing to slide away. "Good shootin', Nathan."

"I hope that woman keeps outa the way," said Nathan, turning round with the telescope again. He moved it until he saw her mount labouring up the steep incline of the trail.

"By God! It's Fortune!" he exclaimed. "What the hell is she doin' here?"

"She's Lightnin's sister," Reno explained in a

192

flat voice.

"What!" yelled Nathan. "Fortune Sarrat is Lightnin' Floyd's sister! You knew it all the time an' you never goddam told me! An' you knew they'd be meetin' here at the Backsight Pass..."

"The word did reach me," Reno said. "So what. We're gonna nail the most wanted man in two States."

"But... but, Fortune. I can't turn her brother in."

"You can... an' you will," said Reno with a dangerous softness in his voice. "You ain't still carryin' a flame for her, are you? A saloon-keepin' girl like that. Ever tried to work out how many guys she's had since you worked at the Wheel?"

"Shut up, Reno," Nathan cried. "You ain't got feelin's... you're just a damn killin' machine."

Reno laughed.

"I figured you were learnin' to be smart, boy," he said. "Women make you think you mean somethin' to them, but that is just their way of gettin'[1] what they want. Fortune maybe sweet-talked you a bit a year ago, an' you're still gone on her ... so gone on her you'd let Lightnin' Floyd 'get away. I guess Charley Donohue was gone on her at one time, too."

A dark flush spread over Nathan's features.

"I guess Donohue got what was comin' to him," he muttered,

"Accordin' to Fortune's story – the story she told you, boy. But did you ever get the story from Donohue?"

There was a silence. From the east Lightning Floyd steadily cantered towards the pass. From the

193

west Fortune Sarrat urged her panting mount up the final stretch of the incline.

"You'd better think fast, boy," said Reno. "You gotta make your mind up. You can go two ways – Fortune's or mine."

A series of pictures flashed through Nathan's mind. Again he saw the tall bounty hunter as he had first seen him, an imposing silhouette against the glory of the sunset on the Red Buttes trail. He saw him with the smoking gun in his hand after he had rescued Nathan from hanging, he saw him riding hell-for-leather after Chet Webb... Again Nathan remembered the pride he felt in himself as he would ride into a new town beside Reno and feel all eyes turn to them with suspicious respect; and again he remembered the almost tender way Reno had taken the gold watch from the corpse of Jake Kelly. Suddenly he saw Red Buttes. The endless work and boredom struck him again, making him feel almost sick. Hannibal Reno had replaced that.

He had turned a surly hick into a confident young man who got written up in the papers, who had money in the bank and black silk shirts to wear.

"Okay, Reno," Nathan said. "We're still pards. But take Lightnin' so he can stand trial fair an' square. I don't want his blood on my hands."

"Don't worry," Reno replied. "We want the second half of the reward." He slipped out of view, climbing down to the trail below.

The ambush at Backsight Pass happened very quickly. Gritting his teeth from the hurt of the bullet wound in his back, Lightning entered the pass. At the far end he saw a figure on horseback, and his grimace of pain turned to a grin of pleasure. There was

Fortune all right. Now his troubles would be over.

At that moment there was the boom of a heavy gun and his horse seemed to fall away beneath him. Next second he was picking himself up from the stony trail, trying to dodge the frenzied hooves of his dying mount.

"Hands high, Lightnin'," came a voice. Lightning looked up and saw that a tall man in black had emerged from behind a boulder. He held a pistol in his hand and there was something deadly about him that Lightning recognised as the hallmark of the born killer.

Lightning Floyd backed away from his horse.

"This a stick-up?" he yelled, hoping to play for time. His quick eyes had already seen a pile of rubble to one side of the trail which would give him cover. He began to edge towards it.

"You're covered from above as well, Floyd," Reno cried, his voice echoing between the walls of the pass. He raised his left hand and touched the tinted glasses he wore.

Lightning continued to edge slowly to the trailside. Reno did not seem to notice him. There was something odd about the way he, stood in the middle of the pass. The young bank robber suddenly realised that the bounty hunter's Colt was no longer pointing straight at him. He had moved out of the line of fire and Reno had not noticed. Without understanding, Lightning obeyed an instinctive voice which told him to draw and fire. His hand snaked down to his Frontier Colt. A split second later it spat flame and the .44 bullet thudded into Reno's body.

He fired in reply, but his bullet went several yards wide. He moved his gun from side to side as though not sure where to fire. Lightning fired again. Blood appeared from a graze on Reno's neck. It made him turn so that he faced away from his enemy.

"Nathan," he shouted in an agonised voice. "My eyes ..." He staggered like a drunkard, his gun firing wildly – hopelessly – in all directions.

The shooting happened so quickly it took Nathan by surprise. It took him several seconds to realise that Reno had lost his sight at a critical moment and was now being shot to pieces. He had not had time to reload the Sharps-Borchardt after shooting Lightning's horse, so he leapt to his feet with his Peacemaker in his hand.

He fired once, and Lightning dived for cover behind the heap of stones.

Below, in the middle of the pass, Hannibal Reno was sprawled face-down. Nathan gave a cry of dismay and began scrambling from his vantage point to his stricken friend. As he slithered down he was aware of the thudding of hooves. Fortune swept past the still form of Reno and reined up near her brother.

"Quick," she yelled. "Take my horse."

Taking a quick shot at Nathan outlined on the wall of the pass, Lightning ran from his cover and leapt into the saddle.

"Thanks, sister," he cried and galloped off down the trail. Nathan raised his gun to send a fusillade of shots after him, but lowered it again. Fortune stood in the middle of the trail. He could not shoot for fear of hitting her. He jumped clear of the wall and raced to Reno.

"Mister Reno... Mister Reno," he cried, bending over the bounty hunter, but Hannibal Reno

196

was dead.

* * *

Nathan leaned on the window sill of his room in the Samarra Travellers' Hotel and gazed down at the dusk-shrouded square below. Groups of people were standing about aimlessly, often casting glances at the adobe brick jail which stood opposite the hotel. Behind its small barred window Lightning Floyd – Floyd Sartat, to give him his christened name – lay on a bunk smoking endless hand-rolled cigarettes.

Earlier on in the day Nathan had brought him into Samarra, where he would stand trial for his latest robbery. The arrival of the two men had been a sensation that the townsfolk would long remember. They had watched in silence as Lightning, his hands tied behind his back and a bloodied bandage round his body, sat astride a horse led by a gaunt-looking, young man in dusty black.

They had halted in silence before the office of the town marshal and as that worthy had come out Nathan merely said: "Here's your man, Marshal." He tossed him the reins of the lead horse.

"Be seein' you, Lightning," he added to the prisoner and then rode slowly to the corral at the back of the Travellers' Hotel.

He heard the whispers of the onlookers: "Say, ain't that Nathan Knight... Reno's pal... bounty hunter ... shot down Charley Donohue over Gila way ... mighty fast... straightest shot in the state ... did you hear about him at Crazy Steer ford? ... dangerous *hombre* ..."

Once such words would have brought a good feeling to the young man. He had enjoyed being recognised and pointed out as a *somebody,* but now his thoughts were sombre.

The capture of Lightning had been easy. After he had realised Reno was beyond human aid, Nathan collected his rifle and had begun the pursuit on his faithful black mare.

Fortune had tried to block his way, a look of pleading on her face.

"I ain't aimin' on killin' him," he'd said. "That'd be too quick. He's gonna stand trial."

After some hard galloping he'd overtaken Lightning enough to get him within range of the Sharps-Borchardt. He had halted his mare, taken careful aim and once again Lightning's horse was shot from under him. The young bank robber was catapulted from his saddle, striking his head against a large stone. When he opened his eyes he found he was disarmed and Nathan was carefully bandaging the wound in his back which had started to bleed again.

"I guess you win," he muttered.

"Looks like it, Lightnin'," said Nathan.

"I'm sorry about your buddy," Lightning remarked presently.

"There was no hard feelin's about it."

"I guess there wasn't," Nathan said. "But he's dead just the same."

Nathan finished tying the knots of the bandage and then sat for a while at the edge of the trail, watching his prisoner with a curious expression.

"So what now?" asked Lightning. "Must say I'm kinda surprised you ain't put a bullet through me. I've heard tell you was pretty close with Reno."

"Yeah, I guess he meant a lot to me," said Nathan thoughtfully. "Anyways, I'm gonna take you to Samarra. You can stand trial fair an' square."

"What about my sister – Fortune?"

"I guess she'll be able to see you in Samarra."

"Poor kid. I guess I ain't helped her life much. I figured she was okay with her own gamblin' set-up ... never thought much about her until I got this bullet in me at Samarra. Goddam banks, they're the cause of all our grief."

"How d'you feel?"

"My head feels like its got a mission bell inside it, an' that wound ain't exactly pleasant, but otherwise I reckon I'm okay."

"Good. I'll get Reno's hoss an' we'll start the trail to Samarra."

"Take your time," Lightning grinned weakly. "I ain't in no hurry."

On the journey to Samarra, Nathan, to his surprise, found that he rather liked his prisoner. Once or twice he even found himself laughing at a joke with him. He had never shared a joke with Reno. He suddenly realised that the bounty hunter had possessed no sense of humour.

Once, when they were sitting by a small fire while Nathan cooked a pannikin of beans, Lightning said: "One thing I could never figure out about you guys ..."

"What's that?"

"Waal, don't take it wrong, but the fact that you could shoot down guys jest for money. It weren't as if you had anything personal against 'em. You didn't hate 'em, yet you could draw a bead . . ."

"Yeah," said Nathan softly. "I'm just startin' to wonder about it myself."

Now, looking down on the square and the jail, his thoughts weje with the prisoner. It was funny, but under different circumstances he felt they could have been friends. He'd never had a friend near his own age. Mister Reno had been quite a lot older... He suddenly realised that he still thought of the dead bounty hunter as *Mister* Reno. Had he and Reno been friends? Surely you don't think of a friend as "mister." And yet Hannibal Reno had meant so much to him.

Suddenly he saw a familiar figure moving across the square towards the hotel. The people moved back to make a way for her. Their talk died as she was recognised as the famous Fortune, the sister of the prisoner.

"Fortune," called Nathan. She looked up briefly and then entered the hotel. Even though the dusk was thickening Nathan recognised the look of hatred on her face.

Disconsolately he turned back into his room and threw himself down on his bed.

Someone had begun to shout in the square. The words flowed in through the open window.

" 'Tain't no point in waitin' fer a judge ... gotta show these thugs that Samarra ain't easy pickin's... the law's too slow ... our own justice ..."

A frantic knocking at the door roused Nathan from a confused sleep. A babble of noise came from the square outside and the ruddy glow of torches reflected on the walls of his room.

He opened the door and Fortune rushed in.

"Nathan," she cried. "They're going to lynch Floyd." She collapsed on the bed in a flood of tears.

"What?" cried Nathan, springing to the window. The square was a sea of dark heads, over which tar-soaked pieces of wood flared dramatically

200

as the mob waved them too and fro. As Nathan looked he saw the town marshal standing at the door of the jail with a shotgun in his hands.

"Give him up, marshal," cried a harsh voice, louder than the rest. "We'll do the judge's job for him." There was a deep chorus of agreement. The marshal tried to speak but his words were drowned in the angry roar of the mob.

"Any minute they'll drag him from the jail and ... and lynch him," cried Fortune. "I hated you for capturing him, Nathan, but now you are my only hope. And if it's the reward... I'll make it up to you."

"Goddam it, Fortune," cried Nathan, seizing her roughly by the shoulders, "I don't give a cuss for the reward. I guess I never did, I just wanted to follow Reno. Now, listen, go to the corral..."

A minute later Fortune left by the back door of the hotel while Nathan buckled on his gunbelt. The noise from the square had increased, and above the .shouting there came the crash of a heavy log being battered against the door of the jail. Suddenly there was a wild yell of triumph as it collapsed and the mob streamed in.

Nathan returned to the window. Directly below it was the roof of a verandah which ran along the front of the Travellers' Hotel, Carefully he climbed out of the window and stood on the roof, looking down at the confused scene below.

Another roar went up from the mob as Nathan saw Lightning dragged by his arms from the jail. He was hustled to a corner of the square where a rope had been tossed over the crossbar of a telegraph pole. There was a struggle as the leader of the lynch

201

mob tried to get the noose over Lightning's head.

At that moment Nathan fired into the air. The sharp retort of the Peacemaker cut through the noise like a knife. Slowly the faces of the crowd turned to see the figure of Nathan on the verandah above them. In his black clothes he looked strangely sinister in the flickering glow of the torches.

"I am Nathan Knight," he shouted. "I brought in Lightnin' Floyd today, but I did not bring him in for you coyotes to lynch."

The mob listened in silence.

"For a year I've hunted down murderers an' outlaws," Nathan continued, his pistol moving menacingly above the crowd. "But when I see you so-called respectable folk howlin' for blood I figure mebbe I was on the wrong side."

"What's wrong, Nath? Lost your guts now Big Daddy's dead?" came a voice. There was a murmur of laughter.

"I've got five shells in my gun," said Nathan. "That means in the next minute five of you sons-of-bitches could die. If you don't want that to happen take that noose off Lightnin's head, an' let him walk round to the corral."

"I'll see you in hell first," cried the mob leader from where he stood under the makeshift gallows. Nathan could see him clearly in the light of a torch. He saw him pull a gun from his waistband and raise it.

Nathan's Colt exploded again. The man gave a sob of pain and dropped to his knees. Those near him moved away as though in fear of being contaminated by his ill fortune. Lightning was left standing alone.

"Make for the corral," called Nathan. "I'll hold these justice-lovin' folk back."

Lightning walked forward and a path appeared before him magically. Nathan watched in silence as the young man crossed the square and disappeared round the corner of the hotel.

"Anyone that tries to follow will know what to expect," Nathan said. He threw his leg over the window sill and climbed back into his room.

Immediately there was uproar outside, but it ceased as he fired a random shot out of the window. Inside the hotel he raced down the stairs and out of the back door. Here Lightning and Fortune were waiting in their saddles. Fortune held the reins of Nathan's mare.

He swung up into the saddle, and next moment the trio were off, galloping through the streets of Samarra. Nathan fired his gun above his head until his chambers were empty to discourage any pursuit. Soon they were riding hard across the open plain.

"Where are we headin'?" yelled Lightning.

"South. South to the border," cried Fortune.

* * *

It was sunset. All through the day the fugitives had ridden their weary mounts and now they allowed the animals to walk. About them the terrain had changed from the plain, with its covering of bunch grass, to an arid landscape of desert where the only vegetation was withered clumps of chaparral and the majestic saguaros which stood like kings of the barren land.

"I guess this is where the trail forks," said Nathan.

203

"Yes," said Fortune. "What are you going to do?"

"I don't know," Nathan admitted. "In helpin' a prisoner to escape I guess I've put myself on the wrong side of the law."

"But it was a lynch mob," Fortune said.

"Sure, but I guess I should deliver him up again to the proper authorities," Nathan replied with a slight grin. "But I'm out of that trade now. My bounty huntin' days died with Reno."

"I'm glad," murmured Fortune.

"Why not come with me," said Lightning. "There's many a bank ..."

"That'd be jest changin' one side for another. Nope, I guess I'll jest mosey along. Maybe I oughta go back to farmin'." He laughed slightly, then looked at Fortune.

"Good luck down south," he said at length.

"She don't need to go south," exclaimed Lightning. "I'm the only one here with a price on my head. So, thanks for everythin' ... both of you." He touched his horse's flanks with his spurs and cantered off along the trail which led towards the border.

For a while they could hear the drumming of his horse's hooves, then all was silence. The dying sun threw long shadows and purple night began to gather over the desert.

"It looks like we'll be sharin' a trail for a while," said Nathan at last.

"A sundown trail . . ." murmured Fortune. As she spoke, her head turned to Nathan, the lurid light of the low sun caught her face between its long tresses of black hair. Nathan felt his breath catch at her beauty, yet her words suddenly brought back a vision of Reno as he rode towards Nathan along the Red Buttes trail, with the sunset flaring behind him, over a year ago.

"He was a strange man," Nathan mused, but Fortune did not hear him. She had already started along the trail.